FAVOR

Steven x Davis

ISBN-10: 0-615-96013-8
ISBN-13: 978-0-615-96013-5

This book is dedicated to all
the mathematicians and computer scientists
who believed in me before
I abandoned them to become a writer.

Chapter One

My first day in Hell was the worst. When I went to pick up my visitor's pass at the office, I had to wait almost 45 minutes before I got called in.

Everyone else in the waiting room had clipboards and pencils. They were all diligently filling out their paperwork, but occasionally they'd stop and glare at me. I peeked at one form to see a few of the questions:

"Which word best describes your most severe iniquity?"

"On a scale of 1 to 10, what is your current level of repentance?

"How frequently do you pray or complete a prayer-like ritual?"

I didn't have anything else to do, so I read the two magazines on the table. One was a pamphlet critiquing death metal bands, the other was burlesque pornography. There was also a newspaper from 1997, but someone had already done the crossword.

Most of the damned souls got called ahead of me, including one who had arrived after I did. I was pretty irate when the receptionist finally called my name.

"Douglas DeWitt?"

I walked up to the desk.

"You'll be in Consultation Room 3," she said. "Go through that door and take the second right. It's down the hallway about six miles. On the left." She flipped a switch and the automatic door opened.

"Don't forget your rucksack."

I muttered that it was called a backpack and went to get it. After I put it on and buckled the waist strap, I headed through the door.

The "hallway" was more of a dingy tunnel than anything else. The walls were blank gray stone; the background music was easy listening interspersed with a chorus of screams. The stench of rubbing alcohol wafted through the air.

There were a few office doors on the left and several tunnels opening to the right. A wooden signpost by the second hallway said "Consultation Rooms 1 to 3330." I started down it.

All the doors were on the left. Beside each one was a plain white placard with a number. Naturally, they were in descending order.

After I trudged past about 300 rooms, I stopped trying to calculate how much longer it would take. I didn't encounter anyone else in the hallway, but I saw two employee break rooms along the way. They were both locked tight.

I finally reached Consultation Room 3, the last door on the left. Consultation Rooms 1 and 2 didn't seem to exist. I caught my breath and steeled myself for a demonic confrontation. When I felt I was ready, I swung the door open and went inside.

The consultation room was brightly lit and sterile. A large computer desk took up most of the space. There was a luxurious office chair on the other side and a small wooden stool for me, both vacant.

When I sat down, my knees were at chest-level. I looked at the posters on the wall while I waited for the consultant to arrive. They all featured the caption "Hang in There!" under various photographs of animals dangling from trees.

I was looking at a raccoon when the door behind me finally opened and a reddish-purple succubus walked in.

She was tall, especially from my current vantage point. Her black hair was tied into a bun, and she was wearing a skimpy business suit with a bare midriff. On top of her absurdly-large bosom was a nametag: "Bordella." Her tiny bat wings and eyeglasses were clearly just for show.

"Hello, Mr. DeWitt," she said. She walked around the desk and sat down. "May I call you Douglas?"

"Just Doug."

"Of course. I'm going to call up your file on the computer. In the meantime, please take off your rucksack."

"It's a backpack."

"Mm." She started typing as I unstrapped myself. "Okay. Douglas DeWitt, 24 years old, 6'1", 250 pounds, brown hair, blue eyes. I assume that's you?"

"Yes." I worked the backpack over my head and set it by the door, trying not to fall off of my stool in the process.

"Now, it says here you're inquiring about a visitor's pass?"

"Right. I need to see Dr. Alphonse Bloom. According to Dante's *Inferno*, he should be in the seventh circle."

She laughed. "Doug, there are no circles in Hell. Why would we keep all the murderers in one place when we can spread them throughout the population? It saves us a great deal of work."

"Well, he wasn't a murderer or anything. He committed suicide."

"Whatever you say." She kept typing. "Let's see, you submitted all the preliminary paperwork, but you still have to sign a few things." She reached into a drawer and pulled out several forms. "These all have to be signed in blood."

"I actually have a pen with me somewhere."

"Is it red?"

"Yeah."

"That's fine." I dug through my pockets as she continued. "The first form is your agreement to be temporarily dead. For the duration of your stay in Hell, you will be considered deceased. We will reinstate your existence upon receipt of your visitor's pass.

"Second, you acknowledge that the visitor's pass is a bearer

3

instrument. In other words, anyone with your pass will be able to complete the exit procedure. It contains no identifying information and is unrecoverable in the event of theft. Replacement passes are not issued. In the absence of a pass, this contract is void.

"Third, you agree to remain an objective observer during the course of your stay. If you are caught consoling or sympathizing with the damned, you may be subject to immediate punishment. Interact with citizens at your own risk.

"Finally, you will hold harmless Hell, its representatives, and citizens for any incidental or collateral torture you may incur during your stay."

I yanked the pen out of my back pocket. "Most of that makes sense," I said, "but can't I just write my name on the pass?"

She raised an eyebrow. "I'm afraid that won't work. The pass is our method of keeping you in check. If you behave responsibly, you have nothing to worry about. If you start taking risks, we don't guarantee anything."

"I see. This is getting kind of complicated. Do you have a guide book or brochure or something?"

"No. The management forces us to let you in, but we're not here to help. Now, are you going to sign or not?"

I signed the papers and passed them over.

"Excellent," she said. "Now, there are a few formalities we need to go through before you leave. Hand over your rucksack."

I gave her the bag and she dumped its contents on the desk. She set aside my water bottles and rifled through the food.

"These chocolate bars are going to melt immediately. The gummy bears are likely to do the same. As for these sandwiches, the peanut butter will be completely runny and the bread will get stale right away." She looked up. "What made you decide to bring a bag of Lucky Charms?"

I shrugged. "Just, you know, luck."

"Right. Well, the marshmallows are going to melt." She shifted the food aside and looked at the gear.

"Okay. The portable fan was a good idea, but the batteries are going to die. The flashlight will work perfectly until you need it. You think you'll use matches?" She shook her head. "You've got to be kidding me.

"Let's see, the rope and the blank notebook are fine as is. I have to confiscate the other books, but I can replace them with ones you don't like."

"Will I have read them before?"

"Absolutely. They were probably assigned as homework."

"Okay, then I pass."

She unzipped the camping pillow and pulled out most of the feathers, then moved on to the spare clothes.

"These are fine, but all your clothes are going to get covered with plenty of soot and scorch marks." She pulled out my pair of work gloves. "Hm. These could be useful. I have to take one of them."

She threw the right glove on the floor with the feathers, then she replaced my bag of toiletries and with one from under the desk.

"This kit has all the essentials. I doubt you'll need anything else."

She shoved my belongings into a pile and stood up.

"Now, empty your pockets."

I got up and started pulling everything out of my pockets. I dumped several things on the desk, including 68 cents in change, four pens, fingernail clippers, a bottle of Aleve, my flip phone, my wallet, and my house keys.

"A cellular telephone?" She rolled her eyes. "You can keep it, but you won't get any reception here, I assure you."

She took all the paper money out of my wallet. "For some reason, people here still seem to value this," she said, "and I certainly can't let you keep the painkillers."

"What if I get a migraine?"

5

"Oh, you will. Anyway, everything else is fine." She started patting me down. "We have to make sure you aren't trying to smuggle anything in."

After she frisked me, she did a rectal search. She told me it was mandatory for everyone but giggled the entire time. She finally finished and went back to her seat.

"How come you didn't bring any weapons?"

I started putting my pants back on. "Why would I need weapons?"

She leaned back and folded her hands behind her head. "Most of the damned only appreciate violence, and there's a good chance you'll need them to help with your journey. You might be able to move around without hurting anyone, but it's hard to get people motivated without a little pain. That's our belief, anyway."

"I gathered." I collected everything from the desk and stuffed it back in my bag. "Couldn't I just avoid people altogether? Or politely ask for their assistance?"

"You can't live and let live when you're dead, Doug. If you need something, you'll have to take it."

"I'll take my chances," I said.

She leaned forward and we locked eyes.

"You're serious about this, aren't you?"

"One hundred percent." I tried to seem bold, but I was starting to worry.

She sat back, looking pensive. "I see. I don't do this for just anyone, but I'm going to give you my personal phone number. If you get in trouble and need help, I'll do what I can. Of course, I'm assuming you'll be able to find reception."

I took out my cell phone.

"Okay, shoot."

"My phone number is (555) 555-5555."

I typed it in. "Huh. All fives. That's neat. Okay, I'll put you in here under 'Bordella.' Should I call you now so you can save my number?"

"No." She winked at me. "We can't take personal calls at work."

"Oh, right. Okay." I saved the number and put the phone back in my pocket.

She sighed deeply and stood up with an authoritative air. "Mr. DeWitt, I would like to officially welcome you to Hell. Let me get your visitor's pass."

She reached deep within her cleavage and pulled out a braided-copper bracelet with a heart-shaped silver charm.

"As soon as I give you this, you are officially checked out," she said. "Your life will be suspended indefinitely. If you're still determined, hold out your arm."

I steeled myself and stuck out my right arm. With a flourish, she snapped the bracelet around my wrist. The sound of hearty laughter filled the air, but neither of us was responsible.

"You're free to go," she said. "Head out the door and turn left. Don't forget to take your rucksack."

I picked up my significantly lighter backpack and opened the door. As I started to walk out, she said, "There's one last thing."

For a moment, genuine concern flashed across her face.

"This is Hell, Doug. Never forget that. People who visit rarely find what they're looking for, but maybe you will. Good luck."

"Super duper." I walked out, shutting the door behind me.

When I turned to the left, instead of a blank wall, I saw a panorama fit for an apocalyptic comic book. Flames spurted out of the ground in a few different places.

I had a long way to go.

Chapter Two

Alphonse Bloom and I met in 2006, as freshmen at North Carolina State University. At new student orientation, Al came across as intelligent, articulate, and full of himself.

During the Q&A session, he pointedly asked where he could find a nearby gym, stressing the importance of continuing his regular workout regimen and maintaining his toned physique. He also mentioned his full-ride research fellowship several times.

After the session, I realized that I knew the exact amount of Al's cash stipend and the location of the three nearest gyms, but I had no idea when I needed to sign up for classes or how to find the library. I was even more bewildered than most freshmen, and Al was to blame.

Al and I were both studying computer science, but oddly enough, we only shared one class: Philosophy of Religion. We each took the class to fulfill a general education requirement, but it didn't hurt that the instructor was young and extremely attractive.

Dr. Cherry was a blonde bombshell with flushed cheeks and a tight bun. She wore frumpy clothes and acted meek, but she still couldn't hide her extraordinary figure or her gorgeous smile. She excelled at keeping the male students' attention even when her lectures got long-winded.

I rarely had much to say about religion, but Al never shut up about it. He was an evangelical atheist, the very worst kind. Whenever he got the chance, he would hijack the conversation to preach his bleak view of the universe. As soon as he did, the classroom discussion became a battle between religion and nothingness.

Dr. Cherry would disagree in that breathy voice of hers, but it was usually a losing battle. Through anger and sheer loudness, he would get her to concede that her position might be somewhat conjectural. He'd sit back, look around, and flip his sandy blonde hair out of his eyes, trying to detect some approval on our faces. Most of the time, we were just eager to move on.

At first, I thought Al was just opinionated, but eventually, I suspected he was trying to prove something. He hated to be criticized and seemed to resent the suggestion that his decisions or actions were anybody else's business.

The discussion got particularly heated one day after Dr. Cherry suggested that religion was a necessary aspect of human existence.

"Without religion," she said, "people wouldn't understand morality or know how to behave. They wouldn't be able to tell the difference between right and wrong. They'd be completely lost."

Al literally jumped out of his seat. "Religion? Nothing is holding humanity back more than religion! Imagine how much we could accomplish without being told that certain thoughts are blasphemous and evil."

Dr. Cherry sighed. "I imagine you'll find that most religions are ultimately concerned with reforming people's actions, not their thoughts. After all, theology is all about thinking."

He laughed. "As far as I can tell, theology is all about telling people what to do."

"It might seem that way at times, but in reality, people are constantly making choices. Religion helps them choose; it doesn't tell them what to decide. That's why the existence of religion has never eliminated evil. Some people will always make the wrong choice."

"People make those choices because we're all just animals,

9

fighting and fornicating. Why do we feel guilty about that? Instead of denying our instincts, we should embrace them."

"Oh, my," she said. "I can tell you're passionate about this. Perhaps we should save the discussion for my office hours." Fortunately for the rest of us, he dropped his argument. Dr. Cherry's lecture continued unabated for the rest of the hour.

The next day, Al came up to me as I was working in the department computer lab.

"Dude, I have to level with you," he said, looking very serious.

"Oh? What happened?"

He leaned in so close that I could smell his cheap cologne. "Yesterday, I visited Dr. Cherry after class to discuss atheism. One thing led to another, and we ended up behind her desk, having sexual intercourse."

I stared at him. "You slept with Dr. Cherry?"

"Yeah. Let me just say this: When we started, she was a born-again Christian. When I finished, she was agnostic." He grinned.

I couldn't figure out how a sophisticated university professor had fallen for Al's phony bravado, so instead of thinking about it, I blocked it out. I didn't want to respond to Al, but he clearly expected me to say something.

"Um. Mission accomplished, I guess?"

"I think you mean 'missionary.'" His grin got even bigger.

I refused to acknowledge his lame pun, so after a few seconds, he wandered over to the nearest occupied desk. During the next few minutes, he told about fifteen other people in the lab, speaking in the loudest possible whisper. When he finally left with his head held high, I got back to work.

As for the Philosophy of Religion, he was a lot less argumentative until she dumped him, then he started up again in full force. She still gave him an A, though.

Chapter Three

The Hellish panorama was actually kind of cool. The sky was pale gray and the ground was slightly less pale gray. The terrain was flat, barren, and featureless, except for the occasional crag sticking out to reiterate the desolation.

I tried to detect a pattern among the flame spurts or at least determine what made them come out. The ground would crack open, fire would burst 20 feet into the air, and then the crack would seal again. At any moment, a crack could pop up under my feet and I would be cooked. It was a bit intimidating.

I turned around to look at the office. There was nothing there but more Hellish wasteland; the office had completely vanished.

It occurred to me that getting back might be a challenge in its own right. It also hit me that I had no idea which direction would lead me to Al.

I decided that persistence was key and continued walking straight ahead. I wandered in a forwardly direction for about three hours.

I was completely alone. I tried to process my thoughts as I walked. The population of Hell was immense, so space would be at a premium. Why such a vast, empty plain? If no one was here to watch, why all the random flames? It seemed like a huge waste of energy.

I was still breathing, but there was no odor of ozone from the flames, so the atmosphere must not have contained much oxygen.

Either that or I was breathing out of sheer habit.

I thought for a minute about whether I should experiment by holding my breath as long as possible. Then again, I was going to be doing a lot of exercise, it wouldn't really prove anything, and after all, I was dead. I decided that old habits die hard and kept up the charade.

I fiddled with my visitor's pass a few times. It was industrial metal, maybe scrapped from some hellish manufacturing facility. The heart was particularly shiny and somewhat blue. It resembled osmium, but that would been expensive, and given the slapdash construction, I imagined they spared the expense. It might even have been fashionable. I wasn't very familiar with men's jewelry, though.

As I was examining it, I ran into a telephone pole. I managed not to fall over, but I did have to steady myself.

The pole was fairly ordinary, two wooden beams in a T-shape with several wires strung along the top. I looked in the distance and was able to count 35 more telephone poles before they got too small to make out. In the other direction, I could only see 32.

I tried to decide which route would be more productive. 32 was a power of two, but 35 was a pentagonal number. Given the binary nature of the decision, I went with the power of two and started following the poles.

Except for the straight line of telephone wires, nothing suggested that this path was more important than any other. Someone must have decided to connect two distant areas with a perfectly straight line. Of course, with terrain this consistent, there was no reason not to.

A thousand other mundane concerns barraged my brain. I wondered how much torture was based on the boredom of walking great distances.

After a few minutes of watching my feet, I looked up and saw a stereotypical Old West town. The telephone poles went straight through the middle of the town's only street.

"Things around here have an annoying habit of appearing and

disappearing at random," I said to myself.

"You're telling me."

I jumped, trying to see where the agreement had come from. "Who said that?"

"Oh, just some wild animal."

"Seriously, who said that?" There was no one nearby, so I looked at the ground. I didn't see any people or animals, but there was a flower next to the nearest pole, twitching despite the lack of wind.

I walked over to check it out. It was a translucent white bulb on top of a dark blue stem. There were a few dark blue leaves on the stem but no flowers. I knelt down to examine it.

It giggled. "If you sniff me, I'll be so offended."

"I don't really want to sniff you. What if your odor is offensive?" I said. "Wait, what are you, some kind of demonic Hell blossom?"

I looked really close, taking care not to inhale. The bulb rotated and I realized that it wasn't a bulb at all, but a miniature skull. Its tiny jaw started moving.

"I'm a person just like you, fella!"

"Well, that's clearly not true."

"Technically speaking, I'm a skullflower," it said.

"Descriptive, but not very clever. Where did you come from?"

It sighed, if a flower could do such a thing.

"Isn't it obvious? I died. Then I came to Hell. Then I turned into a skullflower."

"Is that a common occurrence? I mean, are there skullflowers all over?"

"Fairly common. All you have to do is lie down and give up. As for me, I meandered around Hell for a while until the futility of it all just hit me. I was dead and only getting deader. When I reached this telephone pole, I collapsed. I slid down the pole and right into the ground."

"Is there something I can do to help?"

13

"Nah, I'm fine here. Mostly I just taunt passersby. They aren't usually interested in chatting like this."

"Oh, okay." I got up and started toward the Old West town.

It shouted after me. "Wait!" I turned back. "Just, you know, remember that I'm here. I'm tired of being forgotten."

"That won't be difficult. You're the first skullflower I've ever met."

"Thanks."

I continued walking to the city limits and wondered how much more talking foliage I would encounter.

Chapter Four

My second major encounter with Al came when he taught Artificial Intelligence the next year. Even though we were peers, he was so far advanced that he was teaching a course I had to struggle through. He started the first day with an expansive lecture.

"By this point in your studies," he said, "you should know that computers can do two things: arithmetic and logic. That alone doesn't make them particularly special. They're special because they can do those things a billion times every second.

"You've been told that computers are 'smart,' but that's completely wrong. A computer's intelligence is artificial in every sense of the word. It can add a couple of numbers and make a few easy decisions every nanosecond. No big deal. This pinnacle of human history is no smarter than a 6-year-old. In many ways, it's significantly worse off.

"What can a computer see or hear? What can it say? It sees what we show it, it hears what we tell it, and it says what we let it. Of course, we never let it say no.

"How do we foster intelligence in something like that? The same way you teach a 6-year-old: very, very slowly. You have to break down every problem into things the computer can understand. The simplest terms possible, the easiest procedures you can imagine.

"Most of the work in computer science comes from turning

15

difficult problems into things a computer can do. If you can't turn a complex task into one of those things, it does not compute, as they say.

"And when you're done teaching it, what happens? It becomes a teenager, right?" He chuckled. "No. The computer becomes 'intelligent.' Artificially intelligent, that is. Yet much like a teenager, a computer thinks it knows everything. Why is that? Why do computers seem so smart?

"For example, I could program a computer that could beat any human being at chess. Actually, I wouldn't bother, because it's been done a dozen times over. The logic seems clear: smart people are good at chess, computers are better, therefore computers are smarter.

"In order to get past that superficial smartness, we have to think about how a computer plays chess. It looks at the board position and makes a random move, any move at all, and plays a new game starting from that position. Then it makes another random move, plays a new game from that position, and so on. Whenever it loses, it goes back and tries something else.

"Eventually, it tests every possible move. It doesn't know what makes one move better than any other; it just examines hundreds of billions of board positions to see what looks advantageous. After a few minutes, it picks the best-looking move and it's usually right. In fact, it's almost always right.

"However, it reaches that decision after spending most of its time making boneheaded moves and seeing that they don't work. That doesn't count as intelligent in my book.

"Computer scientists try to reduce the amount of time computers spend on moronic calculations. We can give a computer more speed, more storage, and better methods, but we can never teach it what's truly important.

"A computer can re-enact hundreds of years of chess history in minutes. It could spend its entire lifetime playing chess without ever asking why. It probably doesn't even care.

"In the end, no matter how hard we try, no matter how much time we spend, computers will never be intelligent. In short, this entire class is a waste of time. I hope you're ready for that." He cleared his throat.

"Now, let's begin. Remember this concept: A.I. is search. Search is A.I. It's that simple," he said. To him, it probably was.

I finished the class with a solid B, and despite Al's tirade, I never once felt like I was wasting my time.

Chapter Five

The Old West town was dusty, dingy, and not the least bit original. Except for the telephone poles through Main Street, the place could have been the set for any generic western movie. The lack of creativity was astounding.

I couldn't hear any noise from the buildings and none of them stood out visually. I wanted to find some citizens I could speak with. I figured most people would gather at the saloon, but there were three saloons, all in a row.

I chose the one on the right and walked up. There was a large horse trough in front with several papier-mâché horses tied to it. They were all cross-eyed.

The front door was a stereotypical swinging construction. I stepped through and looked around, letting the doors flap shut behind me.

The saloon was mostly empty. It had several round tables and a bar without liquor bottles. I was surprised that there was no bartender wiping out a whiskey glass.

The only movement came from the table in the darkest corner, where several men were sitting and staring at me in utter silence. It looked like they had been playing cards, but no one had any in their hands.

They seemed to be waiting for me to say something.

"Um. Afternoon, gentlemen," I said. I realized I had no idea what time of day it was. "Or morning? Something." They all turned back to the table and picked up their cards.

They played in silence, except for the snap of the cards on the table. I went up to the table to try and figure out what they were playing.

One man was clearly in charge. He was sturdily built, with a large horseshoe mustache, an outfit made entirely of cheap leather, and a bolo tie. The others were all in modern clothes, but no one acknowledged the anachronism.

After I watched them for a few minutes, it occurred to me that they were just pretending to play cards. Each person would pick up a card and set it down without even looking at it. They were putting on a show for me. I wanted to know why, so I decided to break the ice with a subtle remark.

"This is a lovely saloon you have here," I said.

The mustache man spoke without looking up. "The other two are better."

"You're telling me," said the hillbilly next to him.

I glanced toward the door. "Well, I guess I could go to one of those. My name is Doug DeWitt. I just got here and I need a bit of help. I wanted to ask a few questions."

The mustache man finally looked up. "You're free to ask them, Doug, but answers aren't cheap. You have to gamble for them."

"It doesn't really look like you're gambling. Frankly, I don't think you're even playing a game."

He shoved back his chair and stood up. "Listen, what we do on our own time has nothing to do with you. I'm telling you: if you want answers, you gamble."

"Um. Okay." I tried to think how to proceed. A bribe seemed appropriate. "Just a second."

I took off my backpack and rooted through it. I found one of the

19

molten chocolate bars at the bottom, whipped it out, and slapped it on the table. The players gasped.

A short guy in a trucker hat jumped out of his seat to look. "Is that what I think it is?"

"It's a chocolate bar," I said. "I buy the generic kind because they're half the price and I can't tell the difference. Anyway, if you're willing to answer my questions, you can have it."

"No! We gamble." The mustache man scooted an extra chair up to the table. "Now have a seat. The game is Faro." The other men looked hesitant.

"Faro?" I said. "Why Faro?"

"It's expected." He paused. "Actually, none of us know how to play Faro. We usually play Go Fish."

I sat down. "I know the game well."

"Good. I'd say your generic chocolate is worth 5 answers. That's aces through fives." He laid out the cards.

"Every time you get four of a kind, you set it down and get one answer. For me and the boys, each four of a kind equals one share of the candy. You got that?"

I nodded, and he started shuffling the cards.

I took the opportunity to assess the other players. The mustache man was to my left, followed by the hillbilly in the trucker hat and two men wearing business suits, one fat and one thin. On my immediate right was a frat boy in a muscle shirt.

They all looked tired, and their attention was entirely focused on the chocolate bar in the center of the table.

The mustache man finished shuffling and dealt. He and the hillbilly each got four cards, the rest of us got three. We all picked up our hands. I had a two, a four, and a five.

The mustache man grinned and laid down his hand.

"All threes," he said.

I wanted to point out that usually the dealer goes last, but they clearly played by different rules.

The hillbilly went next. He laid down his hand immediately. "Four aces."

The fat businessman looked me right in the eye. "Got any twos?"

"Yes, actually." I handed him my two of spades, and he laid down four twos. I was running out of options.

The skinny businessman looked bored. "Got any fours?"

"Yes." I handed him the four of hearts. He laid down all the fours.

I only had one card and the frat boy had three. "Got any fives?" he asked. I sighed and handed over my last card. He laid down the set of fives, looked at me, and shrugged.

"Sorry, bro."

The mustache man stood up. "Well, that was a fine game, but it looks like you get no answers."

"Shucks." I got up to leave. "I guess that wraps things up. Thanks for your help, anyway." I started walking toward the door. They looked at one another, agape.

The mustache man interrupted my departure. "What, you aren't pissed off? We just cheated you!"

I shrugged. "Well, I had my suspicions, but after all, it wasn't impossible, just unlikely." When he didn't respond, I continued. "I mean, the probability is awfully low, but if the cards were sufficiently randomized, it could happen."

"They weren't random at all. I stacked the deck."

I realized that the discussion wasn't going to be very fruitful, so I tried to escape before things got worse.

"It's okay. I'll just move on. At least you guys get to split the candy equally, right?"

The mustache man's eyes widened. He spun around to look at the table, but the chocolate bar wasn't there; the frat boy had it in his clutches. The two businessmen were eager to take it from him, and the hillbilly was waiting to see what would happen.

The mustache man and the frat boy locked eyes. Before the mustache man could even move, the frat boy ripped open the package and squeezed all the chocolate paste into his mouth. He cast the wrapper aside.

The hillbilly jumped for it and started trying to extract any vestigial candy. The mustache man shot across the room and choked the frat boy before he could swallow.

I tried to sneak out of the saloon, but the hillbilly looked straight at me.

"Maybe he has more!" The melee immediately stopped. Five pairs of eyes looked directly at me, then my backpack. The group rushed toward me in unison.

I stumbled to the door and swung my way out. They grabbed me and attempted to rip off my backpack, but the waist strap was firmly buckled.

While I was trying to shake them off, I knocked over a few of the artificial horses in front. Their crossed eyes stared at me in dismay.

The men shoved me to the ground and started punching, aiming mostly for my nose and lungs.

Right before I reached the brink of unconsciousness, I heard the crack of a gunshot. The hillbilly clutched his chest and screamed as blood gushed out. The other players scurried away.

A young woman with a black derringer pistol was standing over me. She looked down and said, "Did they get you with the Go Fish routine?"

Chapter Six

In our senior year, Al single-handedly ruined the Christmas party. As a freshman, he had been upset that we even observed a religious holiday. The faculty convinced him that the celebration was purely secular and changed the name to the "Computer Science Department Holiday Gala." He acquiesced and graced us with his presence every year.

Al was known as something of a wunderkind among the faculty. They called him "The Debunker," because he pinpointed the flaws in everything. He could walk into a room and immediately prove that your entire day had been a waste of time.

Of course, if you ever asked him to stay and work on a new solution, he would make an excuse and leave.

He was a part-time research assistant on all the faculty projects, and everybody knew he was the true author of Professor Ogilvy's dissertation. He never seemed overcommitted, though, because he spent so little time on any of it. He only showed up occasionally to ruin everyone's progress.

Even though his assistance was perpetually frustrating, it did help, and once in a while, he would look everything over and wander off without a single remark. Those moments, however rare, represented great success.

Everyone in the department wanted his input, students and

professors alike. They knew that a few minutes alone with Alphonse Bloom were a precious commodity, and the Holiday Gala was a perfect time to get them.

Most of the faculty members used his guidance to stay on course in the New Year, so even the professors who hated socializing still showed up.

It became a bizarre competition for his attention. Al was the belle of the ball and he knew his time was at a premium, so he fully intended to get compensated. His price was female attention.

Naturally, the young, female professors had the most luck, so the other professors started to bring female assistants as a means of enticing him. He would feign interest in the project while staring at the assistant. Sometimes the professor had to prod him into saying something specific.

Al's remarks were always open to interpretation, like a tarot card or a Magic 8-Ball. He usually caught the gist of the problem, made a few comments, and wandered over to another group.

Once, he just said, "Elevator" and a grad student ran off to write it down. She finished her thesis within three weeks, so there was no arguing with the results.

Each year, the celebration got more and more involved. This was the final Christmas party of his undergraduate career, so things were more complicated than ever.

The female assistants were coached. Decorations and refreshments were strategically placed throughout the banquet hall. Mistletoe was hung in convenient locations to encourage dainty kisses.

We had an agenda, with Al's attention practically scheduled down to the minute. Some variation was expected due to the relative attractiveness of different students, assistants, and professors. Partygoers were under strict orders to minimize titilation until everyone had their turn.

We all felt a little sleazy, but the shame was worth it.

Al and I had never spoken at previous parties, but this year I was able to arrange for three minutes with him toward the end of the evening. I hired a sophomore named Stacy to be my date in exchange for Algebra tutoring.

Our strategy was to have her spill a drink on herself so we could distract Al and pull him aside between more significant projects and women. Everything was perfectly arranged when the night arrived, but the unthinkable happened: Al brought a guest.

Apparently Dr. Cherry was available, so she invited herself. No one was quite sure why a theologian was interested in attending a secular ceremony in an unrelated department. She and Al hadn't even dated in three years, but the spark of romance must have endured.

We all knew she'd be horribly bored and would probably stay by his side the entire time. Even worse, she might instigate irrelevant theological discussions.

We reluctantly began the party despite our concerns. All the attendees stayed fairly quiet, murmuring our worries and trying not to stare.

The dean of the department was scheduled to speak with Al first. The dean's prestige alone earned him a conversation even though he hadn't brought a female companion.

"Hello there, Alphonse," he said. "Glad you could make it to the Holiday Gala. And who is your lovely chaperone?"

"Good evening, sir. This is Dr. Celestina Cherry. She's an instructor in the department of religious studies."

"She taught a class I took a few years ago, but we're still acquaintances."

Al and Dr. Cherry both shook the dean's hand.

"It's a pleasure to meet you," she said. "Please, call me Tina."

"How lovely." The dean cleared his throat. "You know, Alphonse, I've been meaning to ask you about a classifier I've been working on."

Dr. Cherry gasped. "You work with classified information?"

The dean shook his head and grimaced. "No, no. It's a support vector machine for classifying images by their content. I just need a less memory-intensive way to complete the training phase. As it stands, I can't obtain any accuracy without several days of distributed computing. There has to be a more efficient method."

Al mulled it over. He was about to speak when Dr. Cherry interrupted. "What kinds of pictures do you look at?"

"Pictures? Ah, you mean the images. Well, these particular images are vectorized diagrams for mechanical engineering applications. You see, the most complicated aspect of developing a support vector machine ..."

We all groaned inwardly. The entire department had heard this spiel a dozen times. Dr. Cherry nodded politely as the dean droned on.

Al was staring at the nearest female student, who tossed her hair very fetchingly. He started moving toward her, but Dr. Cherry refused to detach herself from Al, so the two of them drifted away from the dean together.

The dean mumbled something as they left, then sat down in the corner. He wasn't used to being snubbed so overtly.

The next few discussions were similar. Instead of advice from Al, the students and faculty incurred inane questions from Dr. Cherry. Al just smiled and nodded, thinking briefly about the problem, then the nearest woman.

Although our schedule was still in place, it wasn't amounting to much. Everyone's concerns started growing, so a few people considered alternate methods of approaching Al.

A couple of grad students tried to get his attention by refilling his punch glass as often as possible. They would slink in with a full glass, mutter a few words about their projects, and slink back to the punch bowl. The strategy failed, but their dedication was staggering.

Between the two of them, they refilled his punch glass at least 24 times. He didn't always drink it all, but he went through the punch pretty quickly. After all, he was letting Dr. Cherry do most of the talking. At first.

Al started to get a little tipsy after his sixth glass, but the refillers weren't concerned. They continued, hoping he would be more responsive once drunk. It didn't occur to them that his drunken responses would be completely useless.

His first significant exchange began after nine glasses of punch.

Dr. Cherry was questioning a bewildered grad student about the religious implications of his artificial neural network.

"It's a fake brain?" she said. "Does it have a soul? I mean, is it affected by sin?"

Al started to giggle. "How can it sin? It doesn't even know what it's doing."

She turned to him and sighed.

"I meant original sin. Everything humans create is affected by original sin. I mean, we could be building new minds that are condemned to Hell because of our arrogance."

Al faked a solemn expression.

"You're right, Tina. The mainframes will probably realize they're naked and become ashamed." He started giggling again.

Dr. Cherry stalked off toward the nearest professor and Al followed, unabashed.

The change in tone wasn't lost on us. Dr. Cherry was the one in charge and Al became more interested in teasing her than paying attention to the partygoers, even the really attractive ones.

The two of them walked around the room, sparking discussions about irrelevant ethical issues. Al kept on making snarky comments and giggling. The refillers never ceased their work, though.

After he drank his fifteenth glass of punch, Al made a solemn pronouncement: "I have to urinate."

All the men in the room smiled. Finally, Al would be alone where

Dr. Cherry couldn't follow. If they couldn't talk to him at length, maybe a few offhand questions at the urinal would suffice. Before Al even made it to the bathroom, at least seven men had crowded inside.

Meanwhile, Dr. Cherry went to the women's room to adjust her bun. Once they were both gone, an angry discussion broke out among the people left in the banquet hall about whether the schedule still held.

The dean, slumped in his chair, announced that the schedule was valid and encouraged the faculty to try harder. Then he hung his head and cried. We ignored him.

My slot on the schedule was rapidly approaching. I was worried about the viability of my drink-spilling plan, but I believed it could still work. In fact, it was one of the few options that stood a chance at this point.

Al and the flock of other men returned from the facilities. The various men resumed their positions. I asked the one next to me if he'd had any luck speaking with Al in the bathroom.

"Nope. He just sang show tunes the entire time," he said. "It was deafening."

The currently scheduled professor and his assistant approached Al, but before they could speak, Dr. Cherry came back in and rushed to his side. Yet again, the conversation turned to theology and the routine continued as before.

Eventually, the party started winding down. We were all demoralized from thinking about how difficult the next semester would be.

When Al finally walked past my station, Stacy took a deep breath and spilled her drink down the front of her dress.

"Oh my goodness!" she said.

Al froze in place, then turned toward her. His speech was slurred from two dozen glasses of punch, but we all understood when he said, "I can clean that off for you."

Stacy was under orders to allow this. I moved into position for my discussion with Al, but Dr. Cherry interceded.

"What do you think you're doing?"

"Damn it, Tina!" Al lashed out. "Will you please just let me grope this one woman?"

Dr. Cherry gasped and stormed out in a huff. My victory was assured. I mentally ran through my questions one last time.

With a lascivious grin, Al leaned toward Stacy, hands first. Before he could reach her, he lost his balance and collapsed to the ground. He immediately closed his eyes and started snoring.

Stacy panicked. "You said to spill it on my boobs!" she said. "That's what I did!"

I patted her shoulder. "Stacy, you did fine. This was just dumb luck."

The dean stood up and wiped his eyes. He finally lost his temper. "Why the Hell did we serve alcoholic punch at a university function?"

The party organizers glanced at one another. The boldest one spoke up. "We didn't. It was just club soda and frozen daiquiri mix."

Everyone looked down at Al's motionless body and sighed. Rather than wake him, we just cleaned up around him and left. He didn't even budge.

No one mentioned the party again, but it made Al more evasive than ever. The next semester was a struggle for all of us.

Chapter Seven

My heroine kicked me in the side. "You know, a lot of freshly damned souls come through here, but I've never seen one so eager to get his ass kicked."

I groaned. "I'm not damned, though. I'm just visiting."

"I don't care." She kicked me again. "Just get up, we have to talk."

"We're already talking." I staggered to my feet and coughed up some bloody phlegm. "Or did you have something specific to discuss?"

She rolled her eyes. "Something specific. Come on, let's go to the middle saloon."

Now that I was standing, I could look her over. She was about 5'2", very slim and pale, with platinum blonde hair. She could have passed for an albino, but her eyes were black, not red. They also had dark circles under them. Just like the card players, she looked tired.

The hillbilly was bleeding and writhing behind us.

"He'll be fine," she said. "He's got plenty of blood left."

She still had her gun out, so I had no choice but to follow her up to the middle saloon. This one didn't have any paper-mache horses in front, but there were fake tumbleweeds glued to the ground nearby.

She swung the door open. I managed not to get smacked in the face when it swung shut, then I followed her inside.

The second saloon was at least as clichéd as the first. This time, there actually was a bartender wiping out a whiskey glass, but still no liquor bottles. There were several more people in here, seated at different tables and speaking in low voices.

I overheard one man say, "You know, the other two saloons are much better." His companion agreed.

My heroine seated herself at a small table in the center of the room. Her feet didn't even reach the floor. She set her gun on the tabletop and gestured for me to sit across from her.

"First things first," she said. "My name is Mallory Gordon. I'm a mercenary. Now, who are you supposed to be?"

I removed my backpack and took a seat. "My name is Doug DeWitt. I'm a computer scientist."

"Okay. So you build computers?"

"No, I just program them. Before I came to Hell, I was designing software to maximize output at a styrofoam manufacturing facility."

"That sounds horrible. What exactly are you doing down here?"

"Just visiting. I need to find a man named Alphonse Bloom, but I'm not sure where to look yet. Or how."

"I see. Is this guy a friend of yours?"

"Not a friend, exactly. He's more like my nemesis."

She raised an eyebrow. "You have a nemesis?"

"Yeah, like my professional nemesis, you know."

"Actually, I have no idea. So why did you volunteer for that ass-kicking in the other saloon?"

"I didn't volunteer. I offered to exchange a chocolate bar for some answers about this place. They demanded I play Go Fish with them, then they cheated. I'm not sure why."

"Why wouldn't they cheat? This is Hell. There's no reason to play fair."

"Well, I still need help." I sighed. "I don't suppose you answer questions for free."

"As a matter of fact, I do. It's one of the many services I offer. Oh, but I don't answer personal questions. Ever."

I thought about what to ask first, then went with the obvious question: "Where are we?"

"This is Old Westown. It's one of the central communities of Hell."

"Central?"

"Right. Damned souls show up at the center of Hell. It's sort of the frontier; I think that's why they went with the Old West theme."

"I see. What's the rest of Hell like?"

"Flat and gray. There are some nuggets of activity around, but they're usually pretty far apart."

"I gathered. Why is that? Why not just stick close together?"

"The longer souls stay in Hell, the farther away they travel. Nobody knows why, but I think it's some kind of instinct." She looked around. "Anyway, how close to these scumbags do you really want to be?"

I followed her gaze and saw all the stinky, decrepit citizens. Most of them were tired and beaten up, but they still reeked of violence and malice. She had a point.

"Okay," I said. "So if everyone's so spread out, how do I find one particular person?"

"The old-fashioned way. You find a guy who knows a guy who knows a guy who knows your friend. I mean, your nemesis."

"Isn't there a faster approach? What about the telephone wires? Could I try to call someone?"

"There aren't any phones here. It's the Old West."

"Oh, of course. So where's the best place to find people and phones?"

"The obvious choice is The Big City. It has a large population, and your guy probably went through there at some point."

"It's just called The Big City? You guys don't come up with very original names down here."

"It isn't a huge priority." She paused and leaned forward. "Listen, if you're serious about this journey, you'll need someone like me to defend you and show you the ropes. Otherwise, you're destined for more exploitation and ass-kickings."

I wondered if a tiny female bodyguard would be much help, but then I thought about the injured hillbilly and my bleeding lungs and decided she was right.

"Okay. I guess you're hired. How do I pay you?"

She sat back and smiled.

"Two things: First, I want the rest of your chocolate, no questions asked. Second, you have to promise me it'll be interesting."

"Interesting? What do you mean by that?"

"You know, fun. Exciting. Out of the ordinary. Boredom is a huge problem for me, so I'll only help as long as you can keep me preoccupied."

"Well, I'll keep it as interesting as possible. Let me get out my chocolate bars."

"Not in here!" she hissed. "Don't you have any sense? Everyone in this room will attack you to get them. We'll do it later."

She stood up.

"Now, shake my hand and let's get the Hell out of here. You're ready, right?"

"Yeah. Let me just buckle my backpack and we can go."

"Take your time. After all, this is eternity. I don't have anything else planned," she said.

She picked up her gun and holstered it. I got the bag back on my shoulders and strapped in.

"Okay. Let's hit the road," I said.

We headed out the doorway and back onto the main street. I let Mallory lead the way.

Chapter Eight

After we graduated, I never expected to see Alphonse Bloom again. He and I had both earned bachelor's degrees, but his GPA was 4.0 and mine was 2.6. We belonged to entirely different tiers of potential employment.

My only hope was to get a job as an IT guy for some soulless corporation. I just wanted something to fund my many hobbies.

As for Al, he left to complete a Ph.D. at a technical university in Paris. The entire department was disappointed that he wouldn't keep studying with them.

When anyone asked why he decided to move all the way to Europe, he answered, "Because, you know, French chicks," so that settled it.

The last time I saw him at school was when he presented his senior thesis. It was the only time I ever saw professors taking notes while a student was speaking.

He was also supposed to speak at graduation but never showed up. The university forwarded his diploma to a P.O. Box in Paris, but no one knew if he actually got it.

After graduation, I moved to Akron, Ohio to work for the Darrow Chemical Company. They needed an expert to automate a plastic manufacturing facility, but they weren't willing to pay for one, so they hired me. I earned $22,000 a year.

I began by working with a jaded polymer expert named Norm. After 45 years with the company, he had developed a large polyethylene tumor on his torso. The tumor was hard to miss because it was orange and he couldn't button his shirt around it.

When I asked about it once, he just said, "The doctors say it's not malignant."

The company firmly believed that automation would increase their profits tenfold, but Norm was very resistant to change. In fact, there were rumors that he was trying to sabotage the process.

I started by developing a plan to weigh the raw liquid components. Norm suggested we could save money by just "eyeballing it."

The current procedure required a salaried worker to remove excess liquid from the vats with a bucket. I tried not to stare at Norm's tumor while he explained the process.

It turned out that several of the manufacturing issues arose from similarly contrived solutions. Most of the employees did hazardous, menial tasks with improvised equipment. They were elderly and partially disabled, but some of them earned triple my salary.

Any time I suggested laying off an employee, Norm would rant about company loyalty and providing for their families. I usually had to wait until employees had a serious accident to encourage them to retire with their lucrative pensions and disability compensation.

The worst accident occurred when the guy who brushed out our industrial pipes from the inside got caught in a flood of liquid cellophane.

After he died, we had to fire the guy whose job was to flip the liquid cellophane switch when no one was inside the pipe.

It took me nearly two years to complete the renovation, but I reduced the number of unnecessary employees by 80 percent, and the average number of on-the-job accidents each year dropped from 200 to seven.

The company couldn't argue with the results, so they raised my salary to $24,000 a year and transferred me to a newer facility across town.

I heard that Norm started undoing changes as soon as I left, but his plastic tumor got infected and he died before he could make any major reversals. I skipped his funeral to avoid any former employees who still held grudges.

I spent what little disposable income I had on new technology, computers, video games, movies, and books. I tried to escape the real world as frequently as possible. I also tried to go outside at least once a day, but sometimes I forgot.

Shortly after my transfer, I began walking to the nearby grocery store every Sunday to buy breakfast cereal and frozen dinners.

If I made the entire trip in 20 minutes without having to sit down, I would treat myself to candy and soda. On one of my quicker days, I got there in just under 22 minutes, so I decided to buy ice cream.

The frozen food aisle was completely deserted, so I took my time and considered all the options. There were five major brands of ice cream and they each had limited edition flavors.

After a few minutes, I decided to get two quarts: one with fruit and one with chocolate, for contrast. I put them in my cart and started down the aisle.

Someone else had arrived while I was examining flavors. When I looked closely at the other shopper, a sense of horror crept over me. It was Alphonse Bloom, in the flesh.

I took a deep breath and considered my surroundings. I couldn't ignore him at this distance and there was no diplomatic way to run.

Al looked over, and recognition flashed across his face.

"Oh! Hey, guy!" he said.

He walked up to me. I had no choice but to respond with the first thing that came to mind.

"What are you doing here?"

"Me? I'm trying to find nonfat frozen yogurt for protein shakes.

Looks like you're getting some ice cream. Nice." He grinned. "So what's your name again? I can't remember."

"Doug DeWitt. We took Philosophy of Religion together," I said. "We spent four years in the same building."

"Yeah, I know," he said. "Anyway, you're looking good. When are you expecting?" He patted my gut and snickered. "Just kidding, man."

I didn't have the social skills to respond to his remark, so I had to change subjects.

"Um. I thought you were in Paris, getting a doctorate."

"I finished last month! Honestly, I'm glad to be back in the U.S. of A."

"Right, but why didn't you just stay there?"

"They expected me to teach in French."

"I guess that would be difficult. You speak French, right?"

"Nope. Not a word."

"I thought you lived in France for 2 years."

"Yeah, but learning French didn't seem like it was worth the effort. I usually just raised my voice and waved my arms around a lot. They always got the point."

"I see. So you're here now. Why is that?"

"I read online that Akron is the best city in the Midwest for single men. I couldn't resist." He slapped me on the back. "Hell, I bet even you're getting lucky here, right?" He laughed. "Anyway, I just moved here and I don't know many people yet, so we should hang out sometime. What's your phone number?"

Like a complete idiot, I gave it to him. He thanked me and walked off. I wasn't entirely sure what had happened, but I knew that nothing good could come of it. I shook off my uneasiness and continued shopping.

When I finally got home, I ate all the ice cream.

Chapter Nine

The hillbilly was still lying the steps of the other saloon, vomiting up blood.

"I told you he had plenty of blood left," Mallory said. "He'll be fine in another few hours."

She was right; he did look better.

"Do people usually heal after stuff like that?" I asked.

"Almost always. It's not like they can die again."

"I guess that's true."

We approached the edge of Old Westown. The telephone poles still followed a perfectly straight line into the horizon.

"These poles lead straight to The Big City," she said.

I looked around. "But this is the way I came. I didn't see a city anywhere."

"Well, you must have walked in the wrong direction, Doug. It wouldn't be the only bad decision you've made today." I knew what she meant.

After we walked for a couple of minutes, I spotted the skullflower I'd met earlier.

As we approached, it asked us a riddle: "What has 3 heads and 4 legs?"

Mallory stomped it into the ground with her boot. "I hate these things," she said. She kicked around some dirt to cover it up and kept walking. I was too new to understand the complex interplay between citizens and skullflowers, so I held my tongue. I wasn't really sure what to say, anyway.

After some hesitation, I decided to try small talk.

"These telephone poles are certainly well-maintained."

"Doug, I really don't want to have a conversation about telephone poles."

"Then what do you want to talk about?"

"Why do we have to talk at all?"

"You said you didn't want to get bored."

"Talking to you won't help with that."

We walked in silence for a while longer. I tried a new tactic. "Are you sure you don't want to tell a story or something?"

"I already told you, I don't talk about myself."

"Okay. Well, I have a funny story." I cleared my throat. "The corporate office demanded that we introduce recycled materials into our polystyrene without acknowledging the difficulty of reclaiming workable material from unused commercial-grade foam.

"As you can imagine, the process is more cost- and energy-intensive than we can afford and I told them as much. They responded by saying that the public relations aspect was more important, because we could claim that our styrofoam was green. I pointed out that all of our products are white, but they said to just shut up and do it, so I did.

"In order to recycle expanded polystyrene, you have to superheat the foam and compact it until it melts. We needed to build an entirely new wing of the facility for the process, all so the company could claim our polystyrene was 10% recycled.

"I suggested that we incorporate some biodegradable materials, but they weren't hearing it. They might add that at some point, but in the last several months, we've only focused on breaking down and repurposing old products. As we were purchasing the new computer hardware for that wing of the building—"

Mallory interrupted. "Look, if I talk about myself, will you stop telling this story?"

I frowned. "I guess, but I didn't get to the funny part yet."

"Yeah, I noticed." She sighed. "Let's see. I was born in 1968. I spent a significant amount of time doing drugs and having sex. I died in 1996. That's about it."

"Huh. So did you die from doing drugs or from having sex?"

"Neither. It was a freak accident kind of thing. Very messy."

"I see. So why did you end up in Hell?"

"No clue. I showed up in the office, same as you, only I wasn't just visiting."

"What did you put on your paperwork?"

"Lies, mostly. No one tells the truth on those things, anyway. What's the point?"

"I guess that makes some sense." I gave up on getting any more information from her for a while.

After we plodded along for another 20 minutes or so, I saw a large shadow on the horizon.

"Is that the city?" I asked.

"No, it's just a parking structure. The only way to get into The Big City is by driving."

"Um. I don't have a car, Mallory."

"Neither do I. We'll rent one when we get there." She seemed to know what she was doing, so I assumed she had money.

The parking structure was 10 stories high, and every story was full of very large cars. A couple of people drove out from the first level, but otherwise, there wasn't a whole lot of activity.

Mallory led the way to the rental office in the far corner. There was no line or anything, so they probably weren't getting a whole lot of business.

The bright red demon at the desk looked bored. He was drumming the fingers of his right hand on the desk, and when I got closer, I saw that his left hand was actually a gigantic lobster claw. His nametag said "Craig."

Mallory took the lead yet again.

"We need a car," she said.

"Good for you," Craig said. "I have some you can rent."

"We don't have any money," I said.

"That isn't a problem. Let's go to the lot." Craig got up and started toward the side door leading into the garage. His gait was lopsided due to the weight of his lobster hand.

He pushed the door open, and we followed him through.

"Most of our current inventory is SUVs," he said. "We have a few smaller crossovers and some antique jalopies. Oh, and two limousines, one of which is a stretch Hummer. We have tons of Hummers right now."

"I see," Mallory said. "So what are the drawbacks?"

"Well, there are a few flat expenses. None of the cars have fuel gauges, so there's no way to know when you'll run out of gas. Of course, there's no air conditioning on any of them. None of the seats or mirrors adjust, and there are no automatic transmissions or cruise control. Beyond that, the costs vary depending on the model."

We walked along the central aisle and he gestured to different sections with his normal hand.

"Hummers are a bargain. The radio is always on at the loudest possible volume, the brakes are unreliable, and there are no shock absorbers. Obviously, they run out of gas pretty quick.

"If you want a smaller model, you get all that, plus the heaters will run constantly. You can move the vents around, but it really won't help. The tires on those are completely bald, and you should keep in mind that there are no paved roads, so you'll be driving on the bare earth. Or bare Hell, I suppose."

We kept walking. None of these vehicles sounded very good so far.

"What about the limousines?" I asked.

"You can only drive the limos while your hair is on fire," he said. "There's also no power steering, which makes quite a difference with vehicles that large."

He pointed to one section full of extremely decrepit cars.

"These are the cheapest by far. They have no shocks whatsoever and we guarantee that pieces will fall off. Some of those pieces might be important; there's no way to tell. They also make all kinds of random noises. They guzzle gas, but not nearly as bad as the Hummers."

Mallory and I decided to check out them out. I walked up to the first one that looked drivable.

"Ah, a BMW Dixi," Craig said. "That's a nice choice. Have you driven a BMW before?"

"Just once," I said.

"Well, they're worth the hype. This one is a piece of crap, though. Someone died in it and rotted for three days. The odor never dissipates, but a breeze might help."

Mallory and I sniffed it.

"It's not too bad," she said.

"It gets much worse on hot days." He looked around. "Of course, most of the days are pretty hot down here."

Mallory looked at me and shrugged. "It's better than most of the cars I've driven to the city. We can't get there without one, after all."

Craig smiled. "That's our motto. If you'd like to rent this car, we can go fill out the paperwork."

We followed him back to the office and started working on the forms. Most of the questions were random gibberish, but he insisted that we write something in every blank.

On each of my blanks, I wrote the first word that came to mind. Mallory just scribbled profanity.

We got through all 200 pages in about 20 minutes. Mallory handed the stack of papers over to Craig, who was drumming his fingers on the desk again.

"All done?" he said. "Okay. Here are your keys." He handed Mallory a large ring with more than 50 different keys on it. "One of those will start the car. The rest are just junk."

Mallory sighed and walked back toward the garage.

As we left the office, Craig said, "Thanks for renting! Come again real soon!" and laughed.

When we reached the car, Mallory got in the driver's seat. I got in the passenger seat while she tested different keys. The 33rd key turned out to be the one we needed.

The engine sputtered to life and we headed out on the open road, or at least the open path next to the phone lines.

Chapter Ten

I spent the morning after our grocery aisle encounter worrying about whether or not Al would call. There was a distinct possibility he wouldn't, but if he really didn't have any friends around, I knew he would settle for me.

I wasn't sure what to expect, but knowing Al, it would probably involve alcohol and women. Perhaps the worst part was the horrifying realization that I had nothing better to do. After all, there was a slight chance it could be fun.

I was working at the newer factory that day. The plant was already automated, but there was a still a great deal of waste and inefficiency. I was expected to redesign the software from the ground up. I had been at it for a few weeks already with hardly any progress.

The old system was hopelessly muddled, but I still needed to figure out which features I had to incorporate.

My boss was explaining how he would input data into the ledger with a modified typewriter.

"It's sort of a low-tech process," he said, "but it's tried and true. You don't plan on changing it or anything, right?"

"Well," I said, "I doubt the new machines will be able to accommodate this manual typewriter, sir."

"You could use a scanner."

My cell phone started ringing, so I reached into my pocket to shut it off. My boss shook his head.

"Go ahead and answer it. It could be important. We have plenty of time today."

I picked up the phone. Al was on the other end, speaking at an unreasonable volume.

"Hey, buddy!" he said. I held the phone away from my ear, but it didn't help much. "I had the best idea this morning! Guess what it was!"

"Al, I'm kind of in the middle of something at work." I mouthed the word "sorry" to my boss, but he just shook his head and smiled.

"Seriously, guess! You'll never guess."

"I don't want to guess, Al. I'm working."

"Okay, okay. I decided that we should go to a bar tonight and pick up the two sluttiest chicks we can find!" He started laughing.

Al's idea was actually pretty close to what I would have guessed, but my boss wasn't prepared for it. I could feel his aura of disapproval almost immediately.

"Yes, Al, that's a good idea, really, but I need to get back to work. I will call you later."

"Okay. You better, because I am totally going to make this happen!" He kept laughing as he hung up.

I put my phone away and tried not to blush.

"I'm really sorry about that, sir," I said.

"No, no. I was young once." He sighed. "It did sound important, though." He turned back to his typewriter. "So, you'll be able to get a scanner for this thing, right?"

"I'll see what I can do, sir."

My boss finished explaining the current setup and left. He still looked pretty disappointed in me, or maybe just envious.

I had no choice but to call Al back after no one was within earshot.

"Buddy!" he said. "I can't believe you left me hanging. This is important stuff! I was looking online at some bar called Piggly's, but

I thought I'd ask you what places around here have the most action."

"I have no idea, Al. I don't drink."

"You don't? That's awesome! You can drive. Pick me up at 7:00." He gave me his address and abruptly hung up.

When I finally got off work at 5:00, I weighed my options. I could go through with the plan or call and cancel. If I canceled, there was a good chance he would involve me anyway. If I went through with it, at least I could watch Al make an ass of himself from a safe distance.

At 6:40, I left for his place. It was fairly close by, but I wasn't too familiar with the richer neighborhoods. My apartment was definitely in one of the poorer areas. Of course, I didn't need much room for possessions as long as I had internet access and plenty of video games.

Al's subdivision wasn't gated, but there was still a very large fence around it. Most of the nearby houses cost at least half a million dollars. I saw his house in the middle of a particularly luxurious block.

It wasn't exactly a mansion, but it was easily big enough to accommodate a family of eight. The landscape was perfectly manicured, and the front lights were on.

I pulled into the driveway at 6:57 and went straight to the front door. I pressed the doorbell, and a cacophony of chimes sounded throughout the house. When Al answered the door, he looked annoyed.

"What the Hell are you wearing?" he said.

I looked down. "This is my collared shirt," I said. "They say orange goes with anything."

"Nobody says that." He sighed. "Is that your station wagon in the driveway?"

I looked over. "Yeah. They say purple cars are the least likely to get pulled over."

"That's a myth. Anyway, it's not going to work for us." He reached into his jeans pocket and pulled out some keys. "You've driven a BMW before, right?"

46

"No, Al, I never have."

"Well, today's your lucky day. I'm going to open the garage door. Park that eyesore in there and we'll head out in my convertible."

He slammed the front door shut.

A few seconds later, two of the three garage doors rolled up. I parked my car inside and got out. His black BMW was in the next space over. The rest of the garage was full of cardboard boxes labeled with masking tape.

Al was already standing by the passenger side of his car. "Come on," he said. "We have to get there before the rush."

I walked over to the driver's side. "Is this bar usually busy on Monday nights?" I asked.

He grinned. "I hope so. I want to meet as many single women as possible. Let's go."

I got in and started adjusting the seat and mirrors. Al gave me a funny look.

"Are you sure you don't mind driving? You seem a little uncomfortable."

"I'm more accustomed to front-wheel drive, but I've been told the mechanics are basically the same." I started the engine. "I've also never driven a car this expensive."

"What, this? It was only 35 grand, so no worries. Go nuts." I stared at him. "Yeah," he said. "I picked it up a few days ago. This is all they had on the lot; that's why it doesn't have a leather interior. It'll be my everyday car after I get a couple more. After all, that's why I got the 3-car garage." He elbowed me in the side and laughed.

I didn't know how to respond, so I just put the car in gear and backed out of the driveway. Once Al shut the remote-controlled garage door, we were on our way. Despite his assurances, I drove as cautiously as possible.

"I gathered from your reaction that you didn't know about my invention," he said. "Have you heard of BAMP?"

"You mean the new routing protocol?"

"Yup. That was me." He laughed. "I developed it as part of my dissertation. It's incredibly efficient at getting data less than 64 bytes across long distances. That includes debit card information, so a couple of banks jumped on board. The next thing I knew, I was licensing it out for a small fee. It'll pay the bills until a better system comes along in a few years. Maybe sooner, depending on who comes up with it."

"That's pretty impressive."

"Yeah. I know it's a revolutionary process or whatever, but it's really hard to explain to people. I just want to develop something simple I can mention to get people interested in me."

"You mean women, right?"

"Absolutely. In the meantime, I can always tell them I get a nickel every time someone uses an ATM in New York City."

"Is that true?"

"Nah. It's more like three cents."

He described the technical details of his invention on the way to the bar. I spent the entire ride thinking about how much it earned.

We arrived at the bar around 7:20. The parking lot was mostly empty, but I parked a good distance away to avoid any accidental damage to his car.

"You took your time getting us here," Al said.

I shrugged. "I was trying not to exceed the speed limit."

"Don't worry, you didn't."

He hopped out and walked toward the building. I locked the car and followed him in.

Piggly's was a quintessential trashy bar. It was part of strip mall, but all the other stores were closed.

The interior was dark, and there were very few patrons. Looking around, I could only a booth of five high school teachers, an older married couple at a table, and an unattached woman at the bar. The bartender was playing an old Game Boy.

Al strutted up to the bar, sitting several seats away from the single woman. He waved down the bartender and asked him if more people would show up later.

"I doubt it," he said. "Monday nights are kind of dead."

"Huh." Al got a bit discouraged. "Do you know if there's a better bar for meeting women around here?"

The bartender glared at him.

"Are you going to order something?"

"Sure. What do you have that's spontaneously fermented?"

"I have no idea. Probably nothing."

"I guess I'll get a Cosmopolitan, then."

The bartender rolled his eyes. "Coming right up." He looked at me. "Anything for you?"

I told him I was the designated driver, so he left to go mix Al's cocktail. Al turned to me.

"Look, this might be a total waste of time, but I'm going to go talk to her. Make sure to look, you know, supportive."

"Will do," I said.

Al moved down to the barstool next to her and tried to act cool, but I could see the exasperation on her face.

The bartender set down Al's cocktail in front of me.

"What's that guy's problem?" he asked.

"He just moved here," I said, "and he is very affluent. He wants to use his money to attract women."

"Ah. Well, that might work, but not on her. I've heard all about how she just broke up with her girlfriend after two years."

We both looked over at Al and the woman. He started off with the nickel line, speaking loudly enough for everyone to hear.

She sighed. "This is because I'm the only woman here, isn't it?"

Al tried to play it off. "No, I just thought you might find it interesting. I also own my house and a BMW."

She looked him in the eye. Her face was red and puffy from crying. "Is that really how you try and pick up women? It's pathetic. Go sit next to your fat friend and drink your damned fruit juice."

I turned to the bartender and whispered, "Am I fat?"

He shook his head reassuringly.

Al got up and stormed out of the bar. As he walked past me, he muttered, "This place sucks."

He completely forgot to pay for his drink, so I handed the bartender a ten-dollar bill and told him to keep the change.

When I got to the parking lot, Al was next to his car, tapping his foot. "Come on," he said. "I want to get out of here. Give me the keys."

He drove us back to his house, exceeding the speed limit the entire time. On the way, he complained about his failed attempt at romance.

"How can she not be interested in me? Do you know how much money I make in a year?"

"I'm trying not to think about it." I avoided mentioning that she was a lesbian.

"Well, it worked on European women. I guess I'm just not acclimated to the U.S. dating scene yet. You know, a lot can change in two years."

He shut up and fumed the rest of the way. When we reached his place, he opened the garage doors and told me to head home.

"I have to strategize," he said.

I got back to my apartment by 8:00 and still had nothing to do, so I just watched cooking shows on TV and wondered what Al's next brilliant plan would be.

Chapter Eleven

By the time we reached The Big City, six pieces had fallen off the jalopy. Mallory kept driving while I went back to get them. I easily caught back up with the car every time because it was only going about seven miles per hour. Most of the pieces were mundane bolts and scraps of metal, but the left headlight also came off.

Between two of my trips to retrieve lost parts, I was almost able to coax Mallory into a conversation.

"Why is all the torture so mundane?" I asked. "Stinky cars, long walks, paperwork? So far, it just seems like Hell is just one big annoyance."

"I think it's easier for the demons," she said. "They're too lazy to work at torturing people, so they just do the bare minimum to get by."

"I see. Well, it is pretty irritating. I mean, nothing goes right. Every little task is difficult."

"Exactly. As long as everyone's moderately miserable, they feel like they're doing their job. Besides, they have all of eternity to wear us down. Why rush things?"

"I guess that makes sense."

Before I could ask anything else, I had to get out and pick up a bolt. When I got back, Mallory was as taciturn as before.

She didn't say anything else until we reached the edge of The Big City: a vast network of freeway entrances and exits.

"It's kind of a maze," Mallory said. "I think we want to start with H-616 and switch to H-66. That should spit us out fairly close to the library."

"The library?"

"Yeah. It's the most likely place we can find information about your guy. Maybe you can find a fellow nerd who's willing to talk to you."

Mallory drove us onto the H-616 entrance. As soon as we reached the freeway, we hit a traffic jam. Most of the other vehicles were Hummers; several had run out of gas and stalled. The other cars were trying to weave their way through traffic without slowing down, but it just made things more complicated.

The lane markers were a bit arbitrary, so nearly everyone ignored them. There was also a high-occupancy vehicle lane, but it was full of SUVs with only one passenger. On the plus side, the freeway was well-paved, probably because there was so much construction going on.

We crawled along, moving even slower than we had on the rough terrain outside the city.

"Are there tolls?" I asked. I tried not to think about what we'd have to pay to travel along a less crowded route.

"No," she said. "All the roads suck equally."

Predictably, the other drivers were rude and angry. Mallory dealt with them in a similar manner, even though our horn made a rather embarrassing "ah-oo-gah" sound.

I was glad she was driving, because I could admire the scenery.

The Big City was vast and dark. Most of the buildings were boxy and dilapidated. The styles varied, but overall, they suggested a fairly modern metropolis. I was curious about the population.

"Why do so many of the damned congregate here if they hate each other so much?"

"Some people prefer to be miserable in The Big City," she said, "just like on Earth."

I looked around at the horizon. "What time of day is it? This constant gray is disorienting."

"I know what you mean. Days are kind of fluid down here. When the sky randomly shifts to black, we call that nightfall. When it turns gray again, that's dawn."

"How long does night last?"

"It depends, but it's usually between 13 and 16 hours. Days are about the same length. Anyway, I think you got here pretty early in the morning. It's probably mid-afternoon by now."

After a couple more hours in traffic, we reached the library exit. The jalopy trundled its way off the freeway. If we were a city on Earth, I'd have assumed we were in the bad part of town, but in Hell, I knew every part of town would be bad.

Even though the streets were busy, there were almost no pedestrians walking around. I could already see the library, an archaic marble building near several fractured basketball courts. It had several pillars around the sides and a large dome on top.

Mallory pulled the car up in front.

"Get out," she said. "I have to run an errand while I'm in town. I'll meet you back here in a couple of hours."

I grabbed my backpack and stepped out of the car. Before I could ask where she was going, she sped off as fast as the jalopy could go, about 22 miles per hour.

I walked up the concrete steps to the main entrance to the library. The front door was off its hinges, but the area inside was brightly lit.

I stepped in and looked around. Despite the phallic graffiti and decay on the outside, the interior of the library was well-maintained.

Directly ahead was the circulation desk, where a withered old woman was sitting. Her bluish-white hair was unkempt and a pair of ostentatious reading glasses hung around her neck.

"Hello, young man," she said. "Do you want to check out a book?

The lending period is 14 years."

"I'm not sure," I said. "I really just wanted to get some more information about Hell. It's kind of hard to figure everything out on the fly."

"Of course. All of our nonfiction books about Hell are currently checked out, but one is due back in about 17 months. Would you like me to mail you a postcard when it gets returned?"

"That's a little too long of a wait. Are there any kind of pamphlets or magazines that might help?"

"Well, this is mostly a law library. We do have a handful of nonfiction books in the basement, but no periodicals or fictional works."

"I see. Do you have any books about the laws of Hell? Or are they all checked out?"

"No, the law books are on permanent reserve. Feel free to peruse them. They take up the first and second floors."

"Are there only three floors?"

"Yes. Take your time, though. The library is open around the clock, forever." She smiled vacantly.

I did have plenty of time to look around, so I started in the basement.

Nearly all the nonfiction books were checked out, even the math textbooks. The self-help shelves still had a wide selection, mostly about optimism and positive thinking.

The only book I found in the rest of the stacks was a rather dry biography of Emily Dickinson. I couldn't tell why it was still there, but I decided to take it with me anyway.

I headed up to the first floor to examine some of the law books. As I expected, they were all very verbose and technical.

On the second floor, I found even more stacks, a box of very old microfilm reels, and a card catalog. It was useless because the authors were all listed under "Management" and the titles just said "Laws" followed by long strings of Roman numerals. There was no other information on any of the cards I saw.

Instead of trying to find something specific, I went with random chance. I started down one of the aisles, picking arbitrary books off the shelves and flipping through them.

After about 90 minutes, I had read ordinances relating to lawn care, traffic lights, import tariffs, public drunkenness, pet vaccinations, and mail fraud. I wasn't sure any of those things even existed in Hell.

As I was reading about petty larceny, I heard someone coming up the stairs.

"You got suckered into the law books?"

I looked over and saw Mallory by the stairs.

"They're useless," she said. "Laws used to be important around here until people realized there wasn't any worse punishment than eternal damnation. They stopped following all the rules, then everything went to Hell."

"When did that happen?" I said.

"From what I've heard, about 12,000 years ago. The management still makes new laws, though. I think it gives them something to do."

She walked up to me and held out the enormous key ring.

"Take the car keys," she said. "I'm tired of carrying them around."

"Why do you still have all these? Why didn't you just separate the key that works?"

"None of them would come off. The key ring is welded together."

"Well, did you at least mark it or something?"

She looked down at the keys.

"Shit."

I took the key ring from her.

"It's fine. I'll test them next time. Maybe we'll be luckier."

"Here's hoping. Anyway, I didn't see anyone else here. I was hoping you'd be able to commune with some other nerds, but no dice."

"What about the librarian?" I said. "She might be helpful."

"I doubt it. She's a demoness. Now let's get out of here."

I followed Mallory down the stairs, taking the Emily Dickinson book with me.

As we walked past the circulation desk, the old woman called us over.

"Are you checking out that book, lad? If so, you'll need a library card."

"I have one," Mallory said.

The librarian shushed her. "Not so loud! How did you get a library card? It takes four to six years just to process the paperwork."

"Yeah. Well, I'm a huge reader." She smirked. "Now let's check this out and leave."

"Fine, fine."

The librarian examined Mallory's card and stamped the last page of the book several times.

"Okay, Mrs. Wetherall. Happy reading!"

Before I could say anything, Mallory grabbed my arm.

"Thanks," she said, picking up the book. We walked out together.

"I guess you aren't really Mrs. Wetherall," I said.

"No. She was kind enough to leave me her library card before she moved away. It took her a few decades to get it herself, so she was happy to share."

I wasn't sure Mallory was being completely honest, but I decided to drop it.

"So what was your errand?"

"I'll tell you about it tomorrow. In the meantime, we need to get to a hotel. Night is about to fall and I haven't slept in three days."

"I know what you mean. I'm bushed."

She gave me a weird look. "Bushed? Who says that?"

We reached the jalopy, which was crammed into a parallel parking space near one of the basketball courts.

"Wow. I'm impressed that you could parallel park in such a tiny space."

"You have to learn around here. There aren't any other places to park."

She got into the driver's seat. I put the library book in my backpack and hopped in beside her.

"You said you'd test the keys," she said. "Go for it."

I only had to try 17 keys before the jalopy started. I tried to scratch a mark on the right one, but I wasn't sure it would be noticeable.

"Okay, let's drive," she said.

She managed to pull out of the space in just a few seconds. I had no idea how she did it, but I was glad yet again that she was driving.

"So where can we find a hotel?" I asked.

"They're all over. Most of the ones in this area are kind of seedy, though."

"What, is there prostitution or something?"

She chuckled. "You think they let us have sex down here? No, we just sleep. They're seedy because of how much they cost. You'll see."

We drove for a while, passing several hotels that looked passable. I wasn't sure what exactly we were looking for, so I read one of the signs aloud.

"The Five Senses. That sounds nice."

"Yeah, it's decent. We might as well stay here."

Mallory pulled into the parking lot.

As soon as we got out of the car, the sky switched to black, instantly turning a bright day into a moonless night. My eyes couldn't adjust, so I got disoriented and nauseous, almost throwing up. After about 10 seconds, it passed.

"I wasn't ready for that," I said.

"You'll never be ready for it. Come on, let's go."

We went inside and approached another bored demon at another desk. This demon was more of a blue tentacle monster. His nametag

57

said "Radu."

"Welcome, guests," he said. He didn't look very welcoming. "As our name suggests, this hotel caters to the five senses. You can choose between rooms that are bright, noisy, itchy, or stinky. We also have a luxury room that will leave a terrible taste in your mouth for days."

I turned to Mallory. "Should we get two rooms?" I said.

"No!" She looked nervous. "We need to share. They have plenty of rooms with two beds, just pick one."

"Okay. Do you have a bright room for two? I can probably sleep through that."

"We do," the demon said. "It's Number 115, just down the hall." He waved his leftmost tentacle towards the hallway. "The doors don't lock, so go right in."

We headed down the hallway to Room 115. When I opened the door, a brilliant light engulfed me like a flashbulb on a summer afternoon.

After a few seconds, I could see the shapes of two bare mattresses on the floor with blocky pillows. There didn't seem to be anything else in the room except for the blinding glare.

Mallory walked in and lied down on the far mattress. "This isn't too bad," she said. "I've stayed in worse rooms."

I staggered toward my bed and looked it over. My vision didn't help much, so I felt it over instead. The mattress was hard and lumpy, and even in this light, I could see dark stains. The pillow was moist and firm like a used sponge. Before I got on it, a thought occurred to me.

"Where do I go to the bathroom?"

Mallory sighed. "Have you had to go to the bathroom since you got here?"

"No."

"I think that answers your question," she said. "Now go to sleep. We'll start looking for your nemesis tomorrow."

58

I lied down on my bed and closed my eyes. My eyelids just changed the white light to red, but I was tired enough to ignore it.

I fell asleep in less than a minute.

Chapter Twelve

I didn't hear from Al for several days following our misadventure at Piggly's. I suspected he was planning something for the weekend, and I was right.

He called me at work on Friday afternoon. I made sure I was alone and held the phone away from my ear when I answered.

"Buddy!" he shouted. "Guess what? I had an even better idea!"

"I don't know, Al," I said. "Is it bar-related?"

"Partially. See, I realized that we were thinking too small. A podunk bar with just one woman? That's stupid. Tonight, we're going to a nightclub in Cleveland. I got us two rooms at the Ritz-Carlton. We can take my Bentley this time."

I had a hard time processing all the new information.

"Wait, when did you buy a Bentley?"

"This morning. I reserved the hotel rooms yesterday. Anyway, this place is called Topper's. I read online that it's the hottest club in the city."

"This is kind of a lot to spring on me at once, Al."

"What's the problem? You'll be the designated driver, you get your own room at a luxury hotel, and we both know you've got nothing else planned."

"Al, I just— "

"Great! Come by as soon as you get off. Oh, and wear that orange shirt. I think it'll make me look better by comparison." He hung up.

I got back to work and tried not to think about the many ways Al's escapade could go wrong.

When I finally finished, I went home, put on my collared shirt, and left. I didn't see any reason to pack a bag for a one-day trip.

On my way to Al's, I went by a fried chicken restaurant and picked up a few drumsticks for the road.

When I arrived at Al's house around 6:00, he was already waiting in the driveway next to his brand-new car, a royal blue luxury sedan with a black leather interior. He was wearing brand-new clothes that had been rumpled to seem more casual.

"Go ahead and park in the garage again," he said. "I don't want the neighbors to see your car."

I always thought of my station wagon as spacious and economical, but Al was more superficial. I parked it inside and met him out front. Al could barely conceal his excitement.

"Have you ever seen an odometer with just 17 miles on it?"

"No, but I saw one with 170,000 once," I said.

Al looked puzzled. "Is that a joke? Sometimes I can't tell if you're joking."

"In college, I drove a Dodge Diplomat. It almost made it to 200,000 miles before the transmission imploded."

"Huh. Anyway, this one is brand spankin' new. You're going to love it. Oh, but you're not allowed to drive it unless I'm inebriated. It's my car, after all."

"Makes sense to me."

I sat in the passenger seat and admired the features. Al got in and pointed them all out anyway, not forgetting the heated seats and the bottle cooler in the center console.

"There's also a built-in GPS," he said. He programmed it with the address of the club. "Looks like it's about 45 minutes away."

He pulled out of the driveway.

61

"You know, I realized something today. You're going to be the D.D. and your initials are D.D. We'll have to call you Didi!"

"I'd rather you didn't," I said.

"Would you prefer Double D?"

"Definitely not."

"Then it's settled. I christen you Didi." He grinned.

I decided to ignore it for now.

"I've never been to a nightclub before. What's it like?"

"Loud. Busy. Full of people dancing and tons of women. There's a lot of flashing lights and expensive drinks." His smile got even bigger. "You won't have to worry about that, though, because you're Didi."

His description confirmed that a nightclub was not my idea of a good time. I made a mental note to avoid them in the future. In the interest of conversation, I turned to Al's favorite subject: himself.

"So, are you working right now, or are you just resting on your ATM laurels?"

"Actually, I'm telecommuting, doing some freelance work for a few corporations."

"Any names I'd recognize?"

"Yeah, all of them. Mostly I just consult with their R&D departments about software that's coming down the pike. Whenever I catch an issue, and I usually do, I get a hefty stipend."

I didn't want to know how much "hefty" was, but I had a sneaking suspicion it was at least seven figures.

"It's pretty sweet," he said.

At that point, Al realized that he still knew almost nothing about me. He made a token effort to ask about my life.

"So, what do you do for a living, big guy?"

"I'm working for Darrow, developing software to automate the polystyrene factory in downtown Akron. The system in place is pretty archaic, so I imagine my improvements will save the factory several million dollars a year in waste and shrinkage."

"That's respectable, I guess, but you'll never believe this. When I worked with PNG, I was supposed to review their new method for aggregating consumer survey results. In the process, I discovered that all of their shipping information had to be processed through one workstation in Connecticut. That bottleneck caused delays with their shipments worldwide.

"I explained that they could implement a bare-bones genetic scheduling algorithm, and now it saves them more than ten million dollars a day."

He continued talking about his corporate exploits for another 30 minutes. I was no longer a part of the conversation; I just had to nod once in a while and pretend to laugh whenever he did.

As he finished explaining his fifth brilliant innovation, we pulled into the nightclub parking lot.

Al parked the car and turned to face me.

"Okay, this is important," he said. "It's hard to get into these exclusive clubs, but you can usually just bribe the bouncers. We're going straight to the front of the line, and then I'll give the guy a thousand bucks."

"That might be a little high, Al. I doubt this place is that hard to get into."

"Yeah, but I want to make sure he'll let us in. Better safe than sorry, right? Anyway, when we get there, just follow my lead and don't talk."

"I can do that," I said.

Al got out of the car and I followed, as instructed.

Topper's was an unassuming cement brick building. From the outside, it didn't look like an exciting nightclub at all. I expected there to be a line of people waiting to get in, but there was just one large man in sunglasses standing under the "Topper's" sign. His pants and jacket were black leather.

63

Al boldly walked up to him.

"Guys, I'm not sure you're dressed right for this club," the bouncer said.

"Here is one thousand dollars," Al said, "please let us in."

The bouncer quickly reached out, snatched the cash, and counted it. "Well, thank you very much, gentlemen." He pocketed the money and opened the door. "Look, you're free to go in, but I'm telling you, you aren't dressed right."

Al gave him a smug smile. "That's our problem." He strutted inside.

The bouncer winked at me. "Have a good time, sir."

I went in behind Al, trying to figure out if I was missing something. I got past the threshold and the door slammed shut behind me. Al was frozen in place, so I stood next to him and looked around, taking everything in.

It was loud but not very busy. Most of the patrons – actually, all of them – were dressed in outfits made entirely of black leather. It was a stretch to call some of them outfits, because they covered very little and seemed like they could snap off at any moment.

People were definitely dancing, but very frenetically and quite close to one another. There were a few women present, but not as many as Al had suggested. None of them seemed to notice us.

The non-entangled patrons were sitting at the bar, drinking beer. I noticed that the surface of the bar and the stools were also black leather.

"Huh," I said. "This is a little more risqué than I imagined."

Al's eyes were wide open. "Doug, this is a leather fetish club." He looked scared for some reason.

I shrugged. "That's okay. You like leather, right?"

"Not the way these people do. I think we need to go."

"But we came all this way." I was still curious about the place. "And you just paid a thousand bucks to get in, remember?"

He sighed. "I guess that's true." He looked around. "And there are some women here. I'm not going near the dancers, though."

We edged our way around the dance floor to the bar. It seemed very clean and sanitary, but I still tried not to touch anything with bare skin. The people at the bar were gave us funny looks, but none of them said anything. The bartender completely ignored us.

Al tried to get the attention of a few women, but none of them gave him any notice. I suspected the dress code was very important to them.

After a while, Al sighed and turned to me. "I may regret this, but I have to go to the bathroom." He got up and walked off.

As soon as he left, the man next to me tapped my shoulder. "You know, if you grew a beard, you could be a Hell of a bear."

I didn't know what he meant, but it sounded like a compliment. "Thank you."

"My pleasure." He winked and turned back to his beer.

I wasn't sure why Al was uncomfortable when everyone seemed so polite. I admired the dancers for a while, and to my surprise, I caught the eye of a beautiful blonde woman wearing a black leather mini-skirt, bustier, and knee-high boots.

She walked over to where I was sitting.

"Are you Doug DeWitt?" she said.

"Yes." After a second, I recognized her face. "Oh, Dr. Cherry! Hello, Professor. It's been a long time."

She giggled. "Don't call me Professor; it makes me sound old. Just call me Tina, okay?"

"Okay. You look very nice tonight, Tina." I smiled.

"Thanks. So what are you doing here? I didn't think this was your kind of scene, Doug."

"Actually, they seem to like me around here. One guy even said I could be a bear, so that was neat."

She raised an eyebrow. "You have no idea what this place is, do you?"

"Well, I've never been to a nightclub before. I came here with Alphonse Bloom."

"Oh." She glanced around nervously. "Look, we didn't part on the best of terms. I don't really want to see him, so don't tell him you saw me here, okay?"

She disappeared into the crowd before I could say anything else. I made a mental note to ask Al about their break-up when I got the chance. No one else in the entire club paid me any attention.

Al came back from the bathroom looking pale and sweaty.

"I didn't have to pee after all," he said. "Now come on, we're leaving."

I could see the urgency on his face, so I stood up.

"Sure. These people do seem polite, though."

"Are you kidding?" Al pointed to a man on the dance floor. "The guy in assless chaps has been making fun of us the entire time."

"That's redundant," I said. "All chaps are assless."

Al rubbed his forehead. "Doug, I want to just go to the hotel and forget this ever happened." He walked out with his head down, and I followed.

"I sure hope you gentlemen had a good time," the bouncer said, chuckling. "Thanks again for that excellent tip."

Al slid back into the driver's seat and I got in on the passenger side. He started the car and drove toward the hotel downtown.

"We're still going to stay here overnight. I'm at least going to enjoy a luxurious hotel room, even if I am alone."

"Okay." I paused. "Do you mind if —"

"Don't talk to me."

"I was just going to ask if I could get anything out of the mini-bar in my room."

"Oh. Yeah, get whatever you want." We drove the rest of the way in silence.

When we arrived at the hotel, Al checked us in at the desk and handed me my two keycards.

"Knock yourself out," he said. "It's all on me."

I actually felt a little bad for him as he plodded into his hotel room. On the other hand, I enjoyed my stay immensely. I ate as many snacks as I possibly could and drank almost every soda in the fridge.

Chapter Thirteen

I slept comfortably and awoke well-rested. My eyes had gotten a bit more used to the bright light, so I could see the vague shape of Mallory and her bed. She was tossing and turning violently, making various grunts and groans in the process.

I sat up and stretched, then reached over and shook her awake. She screamed, punched me in the face, and leapt to her feet.

"Thank you," she said, panting heavily.

"Happy to help," I said.

I tried to determine if anything in my face was broken. Fortunately, she only managed to hit my cheek, but she hadn't held back.

"I think that's going to bruise. Will it go away?"

"Give it a few hours. Let's get out of here."

She grabbed my arm and pulled me out of the room.

The hotel hallway was blissfully dim. We both rubbed our eyes until the bright spots went away. I could already feel my face swelling up.

"Is there any particular reason you woke up so violently?" I asked.

"Just nightmares."

"I've never seen nightmares like that before."

"Well, you're new here." She still looked tired.

"Is that all you're going to tell me? I feel like my face deserves a better explanation."

"Fine." She was too shaken up to lie. "You mentioned that things around here are pretty mundane, but that's only during the day. They save the real torture for your dreams, and they don't hold back."

"How long do the dreams last?"

"Days. At least it feels that way. If no one else wakes me up, I have to find a way to kill myself. It's the only thing that can shock me awake." She regained some of her composure. "Anyway, I'm awake now, so we can get to work. I scheduled a meeting today."

She walked off without even looking at me, and I followed her out. As we passed the front desk, the blue demon waved at us with a few of his tentacles.

"I hope you enjoyed your stay at The Five Senses," he said. "Come back anytime."

Outside, the sky was gray again. It didn't seem as bright today, but my eyesight was still a bit off.

"Maybe we should stay in a noisy room next time," I said.

"Maybe. I'm never doing the stinky one again, though. I smelled like skunk spray for weeks."

"I can imagine."

She got in the driver's seat and looked at the keys.

"You marked one, right?" she said.

"Yeah. It's got an 'X' marked on the side."

"They all have that."

She showed me the keys. All of them had exactly the same scratch I had made the day before.

"I can try them again, but you're going next time," she said. The car started on the 25th key Mallory tried. "At least it still starts."

"We could just leave the keys in the ignition next time."

"Are you kidding? Either the battery would die or someone would steal it out of general principle."

We pulled out of the parking lot, bouncing around as usual.

69

"Okay, the guy we're meeting is named Paul Baker. He's going to help you fit in around here so hopefully you won't get your ass kicked again."

"Is he a behavioral therapist or something?"

"No, he's more of a hairdresser. Paul also knows just about all the permanent residents in The Big City, so he might be able to help you find your guy."

"Sounds like a good idea."

"I thought so, too. Anyway, his studio is across town, so we have to get back on the freeway. This time we're cutting across on H-71. Hopefully it will just take a couple of hours."

"That's great, because I've got another story. It's funnier than the last one, I promise."

She glared at me. "If you have to talk, why don't you tell me about the guy you're after? His name's Alphonse, right?"

"Yes. Dr. Alphonse Bloom, Ph.D. He's an expert in artificial intelligence and machine learning."

"Another computer nerd. So how do you know him?"

"We were in college together. He was the valedictorian. I barely graduated."

"At least you finished. I never even went to college."

"I guess that's true. Anyway, he eventually completed a doctoral degree and made millions as a consultant for Fortune 500 companies."

"And you make styrofoam."

"I do fairly well for myself."

"I see. So what's your biggest accomplishment?" Before I could speak, she added, "in fifty words or less."

"Well, I developed an algorithm that was used worldwide in the production of polymers. You just input the chemical formulas and it would allocate resources and notify different parts of the company, explaining what they had to do. That way, the research people were in touch with procurement, management knew what production was up to, et cetera. It became popular because it was extremely adaptable and user-friendly.

"Was that less than fifty words?"

"I wasn't counting." Mallory flipped off several drivers as she merged into a crowded lane. "I may regret asking this, but what's an algorithm?"

"An algorithm is just a procedure that a computer can run. Basically, it's a series of steps used to solve a problem. Creating and analyzing algorithms is what computer scientists do."

"I see." I wasn't sure she did. "Anyway, it's kind of neat that you made something people use all over the world."

"You're right, it was neat. Then about six months later, I happened to mention the algorithm to Al on a Friday night. He spent the rest of the weekend figuring out ways to make it more adaptive and flexible, then he contacted the company on Monday morning and sold them his improvements outright for the sum of ten million dollars."

"Damn."

"That's what I said. Anyway, he won some kind of innovation award from the company. I think they named the process after him."

"Seriously?"

"Yeah. The framework is still mine, but no one remembers that anymore."

"He must be pretty good at that kind of stuff."

"One of the best. He was only interested in using his talent to get with women."

"This guy got women's attention with math? Is that even possible?"

"It wasn't easy, but he did it. His money helped."

"I bet. So how did he die?"

Instead of explaining, I echoed her words from before: "It was a freak accident kind of thing. Very messy."

Mallory rolled her eyes. "In other words, you aren't going to tell me. That's fine. I don't need to know his life story; I just wanted to know what we're in for. What makes you so sure he's in Hell, anyway?"

"He sent me a postcard."

"Ah."

Neither of us talked the rest of the way, although Mallory still screamed some profanity at the other drivers.

After we exited the freeway, it was another ten minutes until she deftly parallel parked us in front of Paul's Barber Shop. Before we got out, she turned to me and explained the plan.

"We're going to go in and get you a makeover. While he's doing that, we'll talk about your quest and see if we can get any information. If he does know something useful, we might have to bribe it out of him. Do you have any other food in your bag?"

"Just some gummy bears and breakfast cereal. Oh, and peanut butter sandwiches."

"Well, that's something. Maybe we'll luck out and he'll like that stuff. If not, we might have to do him a favor."

She got out, and I followed her into the barber shop.

It was empty except for a small, balding man sitting in one of the three barber's chairs. He had a pencil mustache and coke-bottle glasses. He looked bored and a little forlorn, but he perked up as soon as he saw Mallory.

"Hey, Mal. Did you ever find that guy you were looking for?"

She ignored his question. "Hey, Paul. I need you to work your magic on this guy." She gestured at me. "He really needs your help."

"I can see that," he said.

I was starting to feel a bit uncomfortable.

"How are you going to help me?" I asked.

Paul looked me over. "Well, you need to be more downtrodden, easier to ignore, and less like a huge, pudgy target."

"What's that supposed to mean?"

72

"Well, right now, just looking at you instantly fills me with rage. More violent citizens would probably beat you up just for the Hell of it."

Mallory chimed in. "He has no defensive skills at all. You should have seen him in Old Westown yesterday."

"I actually took six months of Tae Kwon Do," I said. Paul raised an eyebrow. "I guess it was more like four."

"Exactly," he said. "We want to make you look more sad and hopeless, so we'll dress you all in black and gray, put some motor oil in your hair, and smear some mud on all your exposed skin."

He examined my face more closely. "This bruise is a nice touch, but it'll go away too quickly. We could use make-up, but I don't think it's worth it."

He turned to the back of the shop. "Anyway, we'll sort out the clothes first. I do have some stuff in your size that's fairly subdued."

He entered a side room and came back out with several black T-shirts and two pairs of grayish blue jeans.

"These are the widest waists I have, so you'll have to squeeze your ass into them."

I decided not to argue and just went in the closet to try things on. While I was changing, I could hear Mallory and Paul chatting.

"So what's his story?" Paul said.

"Doug's a computer nerd who works at a plastic factory," Mallory said. "He's looking for another computer nerd named Alphonse Bloom."

"He doesn't seem like he belongs down here."

"He says he's just visiting."

"So he's in denial. That explains all the optimism."

The wider pair of jeans fit my waist, but the pant legs were a couple of inches too short. I started trying on the shirts as Paul continued.

"Anyway, what's he doing with you? I didn't think you liked

73

swimming with the fresh fish."

"I was intrigued. I'm pretty sure he'll be fun to watch until he gets completely demoralized. In the meantime, I earned a couple of chocolate bars and shot a man."

"Brava."

The two concert tees were so tight I couldn't move my arms, and the retro shirt had a few gaping holes. The designer polo was way too big; it fit me like a blouse. I decided it was the most comfortable option, so I put it on and went back to the main room.

Mallory chuckled. "Nice pedal pushers, Doug." She glanced at my polo. "I like the casual look. Maybe people will think you have muscles under there instead of just dough."

Paul agreed. "I think that will work. Let's get your hair as greasy as possible."

He sat me in one of the chairs and started liberally pouring 10W-40 on my head. My hair got stringy immediately, then the motor oil started dripping on my shirt and arms.

"This will also help with your overall dirtiness."

"It's doing that," I said.

As soon as he had massaged about a quart of oil into my hair, he got out a bucket of mud and started smearing it on my arms and the bare parts of my legs.

"This will complete the ensemble." He made sure to get mud on my clothes as well.

After I was sufficiently grimy, he stood back. "No one wants to beat up someone this depressed. There's no fun in it."

"Be sure to slouch as much as possible," Mallory said. "You don't want to look big unless you're sure it'll intimidate someone."

I stood up and looked at myself in the largest mirror. I resembled a very large Dickensian orphan.

Paul sighed. "I never get to do this anymore."

Mallory cleared her throat. "We also wanted to ask for information about his target."

"Well, the makeover is free," he said. "I enjoy them and there's not a whole lot to do around here, anyway. Information comes for a price."

"Do you take Lucky Charms?" I asked.

Paul got a faraway look in his eyes. "I haven't had those since I was very little." He grinned. "I'll take them."

I got out the plastic bag of clumped-up cereal and handed it over. He opened it up and sniffed deeply.

"These will do." He set the bag down on a nearby counter. "So what can you tell me about this guy? I might be able to figure something out."

"Al is a genius," I said, "but he was primarily interested in picking up woman."

"Oh, a womanizer? He probably went to a whorehouse. Big Jim's Whorehouse off of H-81 is the most popular one."

"I thought you couldn't have sex in Hell."

"You can't. They just pretend. You know, they say the biggest sexual organ is the brain."

"Maybe for some people." Paul gave me an odd look. "I mean, maybe it works for some people."

"Ah."

"I don't know if Al would ever lower himself to soliciting prostitution, though. Are there any other places that women gather, besides brothels?"

"There's plenty of strip clubs around."

"Right, I meant women who aren't affiliated with the sex industry."

"Oh, them. Men usually try to pick up those ladies at bars and parties, just like on Earth."

"Are they nicer?"

"Nice enough, I suppose. Then again, how many prim and proper ladies can you really expect to find in Hell?" He turned to Mallory and smiled. "Present company excepted, of course."

"Of course," she said.

He turned back to me.

"What else can you tell me about him?"

"Al was exceptionally talented with computers. He also liked to drink." I paused. "Can people drink down here?"

"Sort of. Johnny's Tavern has alcohol, but it doesn't get you drunk, just hungover. Some people like that."

"Seriously?"

He shrugged. "They do it. Anyway, technology doesn't advance very quickly in Hell. I've heard there are some computers in Suburbia, though. A lot of nerds live around there."

I couldn't think of much else Al was interested in.

"What about exercise?" I said. "He liked to work out."

"Some people exercise," he said, "but it's mostly out of habit. It doesn't change your appearance or your health once you're dead."

He stood up. "That's about all I can give you. If I do see the guy, I'll mention it next time you're around."

He showed us out the door and patted me on the back. "Enjoy those new clothes," he said, waving after us.

We got back in the car and I started testing keys.

"It's time for lunch," Mallory said. "I know a restaurant around here."

"Is it any good?"

She looked over. "What do you think?"

"Right." The engine started after a dozen or so tries. As we drove off, I looked back at the barber shop. "You know, Paul seemed like a nice enough guy. I should have asked how he ended up down here."

Mallory shook her head. "Never ask what someone did to get here. It's rude. Besides, even if they do decide to answer, they're just going to lie. It's not worth it."

"Okay." I thought for a second. "I guess I was wondering why he looked so sad and bored."

"There aren't any kids in Hell," she said, and we drove away.

Chapter Fourteen

The morning after our nightclub escapade, Al was surprisingly optimistic. He knocked on my door at about 8:30, ready to leave. He said he needed to get back and work on something over the weekend, so I grabbed one last soda for the road.

When we left, Al paid the bill without saying a word. On the trip back to Akron, Al wanted to discuss strategy. He finally asked my opinion.

"I think this trip was a learning experience," he said. "I'll admit it was a little too adventurous. I'm just not sure if this is the right way to meet women."

"You told me it worked in Europe," I said.

"I may have exaggerated a bit."

I tried to think practically. "Have you considered just paying for sex? It's a lot less elaborate than what you've tried so far."

He sighed. "No, Doug, I haven't. Besides, that's not what I'm after. I want to foster a relationship, and sex is just a one component of that."

"Well, there are plenty of other bars and clubs around, right? You could try any number of those."

"I'm starting to get disillusioned with the bar scene," he said. I decided not to point out that we had only been to one bar and one nightclub so far. "I need to try a new tactic."

"You're definitely focusing a lot on your wealth. Maybe you should approach them with something more personal."

"I'm just using the money to lure them in until they find out what a great guy I am and stay with me."

"So your objective is to attract women with your money, then convince them to be attracted to you for some other reason?"

He frowned. "It sounds stupid when you say it."

We sat in silence for a couple of minutes, and then he had a flash of insight.

"What if I could do both at the same time?"

"You mean get them interested in both you and your money?"

"Right. I'll be a philanthropist! They're really just great guys who have money, right?"

"I guess that's one way of looking at it."

"Exactly. When women see me spending tons of money on something worthwhile, they'll figure me out all at once."

I wasn't sure why Al was eager to try something even more ambitious and failure-prone, but he clearly didn't do anything by halves.

"What should our project be?" he asked. "It needs to be computer-related so I can crack out some work between meetings and parties." He stared directly at me, completely ignoring the road.

In the interest of safety, I said the first thing that came to mind: "bees."

He didn't stop staring. "Bees? Like honeybees?"

"Yeah, sometimes they just disappear for no reason. It's called colony collapse disorder."

Al turned back to the road, pensive.

"I mean, all of agriculture relies on pollination," I said. "If bees continue to disappear, the food supply will be crippled."

I didn't know if the idea was any good, but at least he was watching the road.

Al thought for a second and smiled. "It's perfect!"

"It is?"

"Of course. We'll call it the Pollinator Project."

"So you're going to focus on increasing the bee population?"

"Nah. Who wants more bees around? We'll make fake bees, probably robotic ones. That way we can have a little robot bee logo."

"Are you thinking about the A.I. aspect? Swarm intelligence?"

"Sure. It can't be that hard if bees do it. We'll just replicate their method, only we'll make it better."

He turned back toward me.

"You can take care of the administrative crap, I'll just do the science and public relation stuff."

"Al, I already have a job. I can't just quit out of nowhere."

"What do they pay you there? It can't be more than a hundred grand, right? If you run this project for me, you'll get $200,000 a year. Besides, it's bound to be more interesting than a plastic factory."

He was right. I knew he could afford to fund the project, and this would be a Hell of a pay raise.

"Fine," I said. "I don't want to burn my bridges, though. I have to give Darrow two weeks' notice, and then I'll join you."

"Awesome. In the meantime, I'll get the facilities together and start gearing up for our debut."

He didn't say much else on the trip home, but he was clearly excited. In his mind, the plan had already succeeded.

When we reached his house, he just ran inside without saying anything. I drove back home and tried to think of the most diplomatic way to quit my job. I had to admit to myself, somewhat begrudgingly, that I might have enjoyed the trip after all.

On Monday morning, I went into my boss's office and told him I had a better job offer working for a non-profit start-up. It was vague and sounded reasonable, so he just shrugged and thanked me for my efforts so far. He told me to wrap up my current projects and leave by the end of the week.

As I walked out, he slapped me on the back and said, "Frankly, I don't think your scanner idea was going to pan out anyway."

I called Al and left a message to tell him I could start the next Monday. I didn't hear back until Sunday night, when he explained what he had done so far.

Apparently, Al spent most of the week getting the bee logo just right. He had contacted a dozen graphic design artists until he found a proposal he liked and bought it. He also gave me the address to the office he was renting.

I arrived at 9:00 on Monday morning.

The office was brightly lit and completely empty. Al was nowhere to be seen.

As I looked around, I realized that the "office" was really just one large room. The only adornment was a sign on the back wall with "the Pollinator Project" in stylized letters next to a very cute robotic bee.

I had no idea what I was supposed to be doing, so I called Al to ask. He didn't pick up, so I just went to get coffee and donuts.

I came back and sat on the floor, eating miniature donuts and reading until Al finally showed up at 11:00.

"What do you think?" he said, pointing to the logo. "Pretty neat, right? It's like a cute little android. Or beedroid. We can call it Brad! Brad the Beedroid!"

"What else have you done this week?"

He shrugged. "I got this office. Anyway, you're in charge. I designated you to drive this operation. You're still my Didi, after all."

I had hoped the nickname would die with our failed excursion, but no such luck.

"Okay. I can do that," I said. "I need at least one person who knows how a non-profit works and an administrative assistant who can handle the day-to-day stuff."

Al shrugged. "Go for it. What do you need, an engraved

invitation?"

"No, Al, I have to pay them."

"Oh, that. Well, I talked with my financial guy and he allocated 20 million dollars for this project. It's technically a private foundation, so it'll be tax-exempt and everything. I was going to order you a checkbook, but the logo wasn't ready yet. I'll make sure you get some checks with Brad on them by Wednesday."

I had several important questions, but I was a little too overwhelmed to ask them. I managed to get out, "20 million?" before I lapsed back into a stupor.

"Right. You can write checks up to $50,000 without me, but anything higher than that needs my signature. Just save those up and I'll sign them all at once whenever I come in.

"In the meantime, run a newspaper ad for those jobs or something. Maybe you can call up some other charities and get their people. Don't pay anyone more than 300 grand, though. I mean, I'm not made of money."

"I won't."

I started thinking about my responsibilities and imagined the myriad ways this could fail. I started to get a little woozy. It must have looked funny, because Al started laughing.

"Dude, it's nothing to worry about. We'll get this together in no time. We can do a lot of good, and if nothing else, we'll get plenty of attention.

"Now, I have to go home and contact a couple of companies. I ignored their phone calls this week and they might be kind of annoyed." He started walking out and turned back one last time to look at the wall. "Man, I love that bee!"

After he left, I decided I would call some other non-profit organizations to figure out where to start.

Of course, there was no telephone, so I took out my cell phone to call the phone company.

I realized I didn't know the exact address of our office, so I went outside to check.

All I could think was "What the Hell have I gotten myself into?"

Chapter Fifteen

Mallory took us to get lunch at a nearby restaurant called The Septic Specter. Apparently it catered to people who wanted to feel full, so it featured lots of filling foods like uncooked rice, raw potatoes, whole wheat flour, cotton balls, tissue paper, and styrofoam. Maybe that was why she thought I'd be interested.

She explained that some restaurants served decent food that made you sick for days or even weeks, but we needed to move around and it would just slow us down.

"Anyway, once you get this food down, you won't be hungry for quite a while," she said. "It's not like you can starve in Hell, but you'll get hungrier and hungrier as time goes on."

I wasn't hungry yet, but I promised I'd eat something to be polite.

Once we were inside, we had to wait to get seated even though most of the tables were empty.

The demonic hostess just stared at us for about ten minutes, then announced our names and led us to a tiny table right in the middle of the dining room. She told us she would bring two glasses of ice water but never did.

After a few minutes, the waiter arrived. He was an appropriately rude and smarmy demon.

"The special of the day is pencil erasers and agate marbles suspended in unflavored gelatin," he said. "It's served with a soup made from pureed soda bottles and seawater."

"No, thanks," Mallory said. "I just want a plate of raw potatoes with a side of rice."

"I think I'll try the soup," I said. Can I get some flour on the side?"

"No." The waiter walked off.

I turned to Mallory.

"I really need to brush my teeth. Do they have restrooms here?"

"No, we don't do that, remember? They have washrooms."

"That should work."

I got up and went to the washroom, which was really just a row of mirrors over sinks that dispensed saltwater. There were also three hand-dryers and no paper towels.

I managed to perform a few basic hygiene maneuvers, then headed back out to the table. Mallory hadn't moved an inch.

When I sat down, she sniffed the air. "Are you wearing women's deodorant?"

"That's all they gave me in the office. The toothpaste was artificially banana flavored."

"Gross."

"At least I feel a little cleaner." I looked at my grubby clothing and skin. "A little."

"Could you cut back on the optimism? It's irritating."

"Maybe it would help if you tried it. I mean, it's not that hard to look on the bright side." I thought for a second. "You don't have to go to the bathroom, right?"

"True."

"Do you still have a menstrual period?"

"Actually, I don't. I think it's because of the whole 'no sex' thing."

"Right! Just think, you'll never have to take your pants off again."

For a split second, she actually smiled, then she forced it away and returned to moody silence.

After a minute or two, the waiter brought out our two dishes, set them down, and wandered off.

I sipped the soup, which was surprisingly smooth. I thought I could get the whole thing down as long as I diluted the excess salt with more water. The hostess clearly wasn't bringing any, so I got out one of my own water bottles.

Meanwhile, Mallory was wolfing down the dry potatoes and rice. She ate them so fast that I didn't think she could taste anything, but that was probably the point.

After several bites, she started coughing up grains of rice and potato chunks. It hit me that she didn't have any water either, so I handed her the bottle. For me, it was a completely automatic reaction, but Mallory was shocked. She drank some water and managed to swallow everything.

"Thank you," she said. "That was nice." She looked bewildered. "Thank you."

"You're doubly welcome, but it was nothing."

"It wasn't, though. It was courtesy. I haven't seen that in a very long time." She avoided looking at me as she finished eating.

I drank the rest of my soup and burped.

"Sorry," I said. "It had something to do with all that salt."

"It's fine."

She seemed approachable, so I decided to start up another discussion.

"I heard you and Paul talking earlier. I really am just visiting, you know."

"I know you are." She reached out and tapped my visitor's pass. "I've seen one of these bracelets before."

"You have? When?"

She sat back. "I'll tell you mine if you tell me yours."

"My what?"

"Your story. Why you're here. You've got to give me a little more information."

I frowned. "I'm trying not to think about it."

"Fine." She thought for a second. "How about a rain check? I'll tell you my story now. Save yours for the car, when you're ready." I still wasn't sure. "You're supposed to keep me entertained, remember?"

"Okay." I was curious enough to go for it, and I'd have to explain myself eventually, anyway. "So when did you see it?"

She took another sip of water and started her story.

"Here's the deal," Mallory said. "I really did die in 1996 and it really was an accident. My boyfriend Cody and I both worked at a sandwich shop in Missoula, Montana. We earned just enough to live in shitty apartment on ramen noodles and snack cakes. We saved the rest of our money for the true essentials: pot and H."

"H?"

"Heroin." She shook her head at my ignorance. "Anyway, after we saved up for a couple of months, we were able to score two ounces of black tar heroin."

"Is that good?"

"It's really good. We wanted to make it special, so we decided to go camping. Cody said he wanted to enjoy all the natural beauty, especially mine." She shrugged. "It was a goofy line, but he meant it.

"Anyway, we planned on enjoying plenty of sex and drugs, combined with a tiny bit of sightseeing. We took our shitty car out to the middle of nowhere and parked it in a field. Then we hiked about five miles into the woods.

"It was October and the weather was colder than we expected, but we were too excited to think about it. We had everything we needed to use the drugs. The rest of the gear was sort of an afterthought. As soon as we found a clearing, we got out all the stuff, shot up, and rested there for a while. It was fantastic.

"I suggested we set up camp, but Cody thought we should we wait. Instead of thinking about it more, we shot up again. We had plenty of

H and after all, there was plenty of time to have sex after dark. We must have overestimated our tolerance, because we both passed out completely. When I woke up, it was freezing cold and pitch black.

"My watch said it was 11:30 p.m. and the temperature had already dropped to about 15 degrees. Cody was asleep next to me, shivering. I woke him up and asked what kind of bedding he had brought. He couldn't remember, so I rooted through our only bag. All I saw was a tarp and two bed sheets.

"Reality set in. We sobered up fairly quickly and tried to figure out what to do. Keep in mind there weren't many cell phones back then, especially not within our budget. Even if we'd had one, I don't know if it would have helped. We were in the middle of nowhere and couldn't hike back to the car in the dark without getting completely lost.

"The rest of the night is kind of a blur. I remember that we wanted to start a fire but couldn't find the lighter, then tried exercising and wrapping ourselves in leaves. None of it worked.

"Finally, Cody said he'd heard you should get naked and lie down together to conserve body heat, so we did. We ripped off our clothes and wrapped ourselves together in the two bed sheets, but it didn't help much. By the way, I found out later that most people who get hypothermia take off their clothes. Who knew?

"Anyway, by the time it dropped down to about six degrees, we realized we were going to die there. Cody grabbed all the sheets and clothes and completely wrapped himself up. He knocked me down in the process, and I couldn't find the strength to move again. I was skinny and malnourished, so it didn't take me very long to freeze. It was agony."

She paused for a second. "I remember it so vividly. In fact, I relive it in my dreams all the time." She paused a bit longer. "After that, I found myself in the central office of Hell."

"Was that when you saw the visitor's pass?"

"I'm getting to that part." She sighed. "Like I said, I was in Hell. I filled out the paperwork with stuff that made me sound good, but it didn't help. They threw me out on the ground and the office vanished. I wondered how soon Cody would show up, but I didn't see him. I had no idea what to think.

"After a while, I ended up in The Big City, getting worn down by the boredom of everyday life down here. I spent a lot of time robbing people for fun. Sometimes I got shot, but it was never that serious. I always healed up after a couple of days.

"Once I'd been here for about a year, I ran into Cody at a restaurant downtown. He was wearing a bracelet on his right arm, just like yours. His other arm was prosthetic. I was thrilled to see him, because we could be together again. I thought we could at least suffer through this crap as a team.

"He seemed happy to see me too, but he was a little distant. He told me he needed to confess, so we sat down at a table just like this one. Then he told me the rest of the story.

"Apparently, after I died, he passed out, too. Unlike me, he managed to survive until morning. Bit by bit, he started to recover. He didn't need to check if I was dead; he could already see that I was frozen stiff. As soon as the weather warmed up enough, he crawled and stumbled his way back to the car through sheer force of will."

For some reason, the story was starting to sound a bit familiar. I tried to remember where I'd heard it before.

"He warmed up and drove to the nearest hospital," she said. "He lost his left arm and his right foot to frostbite, but for the most part, he was okay. The police questioned him, but they had a hard time figuring out what had happened because he was so delirious and weepy.

"He was able to give them vague directions to the campsite, but they weren't able to find my body for another few days. By the time they finally found it, my body was half-eaten by coyotes.

"In the meantime, Cody started to get sober and heal up. His story was pretty inspirational, and he became known for his perseverance in the face of missing extremities and a dead girlfriend. He was able to recover completely, and then he wrote a tell-all memoir about the experience. He called it 'Cody-pendence.'"

I gasped. "I've read that! It was huge when I was a teenager. The anti-drug campaigns used that story to warn us about the dangers of heroin."

She nodded. "I bet. Did they ever give you the Cody Pendants?"

"They did, actually. You were supposed to wear them around your neck to show that you wouldn't let your friends take drugs and suffer."

"What did they look like?"

"I think they were ..." I froze. "They were silver hearts on copper wire."

She winked. "Now you know where he got the idea. Anyway, he came all the way to Hell to tell me he was sorry about what happened. He apologized, thanked me for my love and support, kissed me, and left. From what I hear, he attained even greater fame and fortune when he got back. For some reason, I think he felt less guilty."

I sat back. "He just left? That was it?"

"That was it. Afterwards, he started using those pendants as a reminder of how other people can weigh you down and pull you into their downward spiral of drugs. Here's the funny thing: he was the one who introduced me to heroin in the first place. He neglected to mention that in his little book."

She stood up. "Anyway, we need to get going. Let me leave the tip." She spat on the table and walked out.

I got up and followed, still contemplating her story.

Chapter Sixteen

The first few days of the Pollinator Project were pretty rough, especially because I had so little help from Al. To start with, I decided that my title would be Chief Executive Officer; Al would be the Founder and Chairman of the Board of Directors. If nothing else, I'd established the nomenclature.

On the first day, I got the phones set up and started looking for employees. After another couple of days, I was able to find and hire two former executives from a local children's advocacy center that had gone bankrupt.

Kathy and Karen already knew how to manage an office and handle a budget. They were also used to dealing with kids, so hopefully they could explain things to me without getting too impatient.

I told them to meet me at the office on Thursday and promised to pay them as soon as I got the checkbook.

Finding an administrative assistant was much easier. On Wednesday, I called the best secretary I knew at Darrow and offered him $75,000 a year if he started the next morning.

He showed up at the office two hours before it opened. Kathy, Karen, and I found him sitting against the door when we arrived at 9:00.

"Good morning, Jeff," I said. "I'm glad to see you here bright and early."

"I'm glad to be here," he said. "Believe it or not, the boss's typewriter broke right before you called. He was yelling at me because we couldn't buy a replacement online, so as soon as I hung up with you, I told him to shove it and walked out. It was awesome."

"I know the feeling."

"Oh, I found this box by the door." He handed me a package from Checks, Inc. that contained four booklets of checks, all with Brad the Beedroid in the background. Fortunately, all of our information was spelled correctly.

Karen looked them over as I unlocked the front door.

"I like this bee," she said.

We went inside. Nothing had changed since Monday, except there was now a telephone on the floor under Al's sign.

"Doug, you told me this was an office job," Jeff said. "Why does this place look more like a warehouse?"

"I've been waiting for these checks," I said. "The order of the day is shopping. Let's just sit down and make a list of supplies we need, then we can go get them."

I sat on the floor and took out a pocket notebook. Jeff and Karen sat down with me.

"I can't sit on the floor," Kathy said. "I have a bad back."

"Can you stand for a few minutes?" I asked.

"No, that's even worse."

"How about you just lean on the wall for support?"

She furrowed her brow. "I'll try." She walked over to the bee sign and leaned against it.

The four of us went through a list of necessities, with Kathy shouting her suggestions from across the room. We decided to start by buying furniture, computers, printers, paper goods and, as Karen said, "Something to spruce the place up."

She proposed several color schemes, but we decide to save the discussion for the store, in order to spare Kathy's back.

The employees and I went to the largest office supply warehouse in the city. The clerks told us to fill out an order form, and they would deliver and assemble everything at our office the next day.

As we toured the store, we picked up everything we could possibly need. Karen asked how much we were allowed to spend, and in the words of Al Bloom, I told her we could "go nuts."

We picked out top-of-the-line computers, fancy desks, and extravagant decorations. We also made sure Kathy got an office chair with excellent lumbar support.

Our official color scheme was blue and white, although there would be subdued yellows and blacks throughout. We couldn't avoid the bee theme, but no one wanted to make it the center of attention.

It was Jeff's idea to decorate the floor and the walls with yellow "pollen" stickers. Karen was so excited with the idea that she wanted to hang yellow fuzz balls from the ceiling, but I reminded her that we still had to maintain a sense of maturity.

After our list was complete, we checked out. Everyone's eyes widened when the tab came to $30,000, but I wrote the check without a second thought.

The checkout guy had to call the bank, but there was obviously no problem. In fact, I think I earned a tiny bit of respect from the employees. Of course, Karen made sure to save the receipt.

The next day, the delivery people showed up and set up all the furniture, which included four desks and a round table for meetings. It only took me about 20 minutes to set up the computers while Kathy and Karen decorated the walls. Jeff put our name placards on the desks and picked up lunch from the sandwich shop.

By the end of the day, we had everything perfectly arranged. The office looked perfect.

Around 3:00, Jeff turned to me, smiled, and said, "now what?"

The truth was, I didn't know. Once I had achieved my first goal, I realized it was my only one. I also hadn't been able to contact Al all week, so I just suggested we take an early day and start fresh on Monday.

We all congratulated one another and disbanded.

As soon as I left, I drove to Al's place. When I got there, he was packing his BMW with camping gear.

"Hey, Didi!" he said. "I met some guys at the gym yesterday. We're going to a farm to shoot some guns this weekend. I didn't think you'd be interested."

"Not really. What kind of guns?"

He shrugged. "Whatever they have. I'm just in charge of providing the liquor."

"Sounds interesting." I cleared my throat. "Look, Al, I just got the office set up and I wanted to ask what I should be doing next."

"Good question. I hadn't really thought about it yet. I was trying to decide between miniature drones or nanotechnology. I'll figure out what's more feasible and get back to you."

"Okay. It's just that we're going to be at the office on Monday with nothing to do."

"I'll come by sometime in the afternoon. I'm sure you can think of a way to kill the time, right?" I wasn't sure at all, but I nodded. "Great!" He slammed his trunk shut.

"I'm heading out to this farm, but I'll see you on Monday. Now move your car so I can get out of here."

I got back in my station wagon and drove home. I spent the entire weekend playing video games.

Despite my anxiety, I was looking forward to Monday. There was a good chance this could go well, and if nothing else, we had a nice office.

Chapter Seventeen

After we left the restaurant, Mallory drove us back on the freeway. She decided that we should check out Big Jim's Whorehouse first, then Johnny's Tavern.

"He might not have gone to either place," she said, "but we can still ask around. I think the bar is the safest bet, but it won't be busy until later on. On the other hand, this is probably the best time to check out the brothel. It shouldn't be very lively in the middle of the afternoon."

I nodded. "Is Big Jim going to be a demon or just a weirdo? I'm having a hard time figuring out who's who."

"Good question. Anything official or essential is run by demons. Clerical stuff, food, housing, utilities, and so forth. Everything else is humans."

"I see. Why do they get to have stores and bars?"

"Hell if I know. I never wanted to open one. You'd have to ask them."

I was getting bored of all the traveling, but Mallory seemed to enjoy it. It was probably because she could lose her temper whenever she liked.

The jalopy was a bit worse for the wear. I supposed that pieces were still falling off, but I couldn't get out to pick them up on the freeway. It couldn't lose much more without affecting its performance.

Beyond that, no one had ever explained where we could get gasoline and I didn't know when the car would run out. Mallory wasn't worried, though, so neither was I.

We pulled into the whorehouse after an hour or so. The parking lot was mostly empty, but there were several Hummers parked close to the front.

The building was picturesque. It had been designed to look like an old-fashioned mansion, and it was definitely big. I assumed it would have about 20 bedrooms, and I doubted there were a whole lot of other amenities.

I turned to Mallory. "How exactly do people pay for sex, anyway? There's no money and not everyone carries Lucky Charms."

"There's lots of ways to pay. Favors, for instance. Volunteer labor is probably how the place stays so clean. There's also the stuff we get for free, like weapons, or maybe you could just barter and get a freebie. I imagine they're pretty flexible."

I wanted to ask about the weapons, but I decided to save it for later.

We made our way inside. The interior of the building was far less pretty. Everything was gritty and unkempt, from the gnarly carpet to the yellowing walls. It reeked of sex, or at least fake sex.

There were several overstuffed leather couches around, supporting prostitutes in various states of disrepair. Most of them were either obese or extremely old. The rest just looked like they had been eroded by years of fake orgasms and neglect.

They all propositioned us, but none of them were putting much effort into it.

"Is this typical for whorehouses?" I asked.

Mallory nodded. "Even the nice ones are like this," she said. "People show up, play pretend, and leave. Few things are so dissatisfying. You have to be pretty desperate to visit this place, and much more desperate to work here." A nearby prostitute flipped us off, but Mallory ignored her. "At least it's something to do."

There was a desk at the back of the room that featured a pegboard of room keys behind a tired-looking man in a sequined suit. He gave us a fake smile.

"I'm Big Jim and this is my whorehouse." He didn't look that big to me. "Do any of these fine young ladies strike your fancy, lad?" He smirked at Mallory. "Or yours?"

"Not even close," she said. "We came to ask if a certain john came through here. His name's Alphonse Bloom."

"I might be able to help. What time frame are we looking at?" He looked at Mallory and she looked at me.

"He died about six months ago," I said, "but I don't know what he's been doing since then,"

"Can you describe him?"

"Average height, sandy hair, brown eyes. He's fairly overweight and his skin is usually tan. He also might have talked about computers or money, although I guess he doesn't have them anymore."

"I might have seen someone fitting that description. Of course, six months is a long time." He cleared his throat and gave us a suggestive look.

"Is that a thinly-veiled attempt to solicit a bribe?" Mallory said.

"It is."

"Okay. Doug, give him the gummy bears."

I took the baggy out of my backpack and handed it over to Big Jim, who pocketed them and shrugged.

"He never came in when I was here," he said, "and I'm always here."

"Fine. If you know nothing, you get nothing." Mallory took out her pistol and pointed it directly at his face. "Give the candy back."

I was perfectly willing to let Big Jim have the candy because he'd narrowed the search down a bit, but before I could speak up, Big Jim said, "No."

Mallory shot him between the eyes from two feet away. I hadn't forgotten that we were in Hell, but for some reason, I still panicked.

"What did you just do?" I started to hyperventilate.

"Isn't it obvious? I shot him in the face. Now shut up and get your gummy bears. I'm done with this place."

I stammered for a second, and then said, "But we gave them to him."

"What did I just say?"

I moved around the desk and grabbed the bag out of his pocket, trying to ignore the damage to his head. His arms twitched a bit, but otherwise, he didn't move.

When I stood up, Mallory was already halfway across the room. I jogged after her to catch up. I noticed that none of the prostitutes had budged. In fact, a couple of them seemed genuinely pleased. I supposed that Big Jim wasn't very popular after all.

Mallory was walking at a normal pace, unfazed, but she still had her gun out. I walked with her to the car.

When we got in, I put the gummy bears back in my bag. I didn't want to lose them, especially now that they were evidence from a crime scene.

The car started on the second key Mallory tried and we drove away. I was still trying to process the fact that she had just shot a man. I wasn't sure if I should say anything, but Mallory spoke up.

"That's the other thing about Hell," she said. "You don't always have to barter. Threats and violence are another great way of getting what you want."

"Um. Right. Will Big Jim be okay?"

"Yeah. He should heal completely after a day or so. Only the really deep wounds take longer than that."

"That doesn't count as deep?"

"Not down here."

"So what's he going to do when he wakes up?"

"Nothing. Hell, he probably enjoyed it more than I did."

"I find that hard to believe."

"You'd be surprised. Anyway, we know your guy didn't go there. We'll head down to Johnny's Tavern. By the time we get there, business will be picking up."

We got back on the freeway for what felt like the hundredth time. I was getting tired of all the cars, and I couldn't figure out how people spent so much time driving. Maybe it was more interesting than staying in the same place.

As we kept driving, I realized how little I knew about Mallory Gordon. I already knew she was an adept gunwoman, a former heroin addict, and a denizen of Hell, but I started to think she might actually be dangerous.

On the other hand, she was still keeping me safe, and firing a woman like her wasn't a good idea.

Mallory looked pensive. She turned to look at me and for a split second, her facade cracked. She looked genuinely sad.

"Doug, I didn't want—" She cut herself off and turned back to the road. "I don't want to waste time. We're just going to go in, get some information, and leave."

"Of course." I decided not to say anything else.

Chapter Eighteen

Kathy, Karen, Jeff, and I showed up bright and early on Monday morning. We had decided that our office would only be open on weekdays from 9:00 a.m. to 5:00 p.m., at least for now.

I explained that Al would drop by in the early afternoon. We had to figure out what we'd do in the meantime.

Kathy and Karen started downloading some business software on their computers. I only thought about ten percent was business-related; the other programs were just cutesy games. I couldn't criticize them since there was literally nothing else to do.

Jeff had brought a book, so he spent the entire day reading. He was supposed to double as a receptionist, so I made sure he at least seemed like he was paying attention to the front entrance.

As for me, I tried to think of things to do, but I kept coming back to the fact that I needed Al for almost all of them.

He finally showed up around 4:30 in the afternoon.

"Hey, Didi," he said. "I knew I was supposed to do something today, but I totally spaced. I only remembered to come down here because I saw some bugs in the backyard."

Al introduced himself to the employees as "the money and idea man." They all shook his hand. Al sat down in Kathy's chair and leaned back.

"So you need to know what to do next. Well, I decided over the weekend that we're going to use nanotechnology." I nodded, but the employees just looked confused.

Al chuckled. "Maybe I should explain. You already know that pollination is when a bee picks a small amount of pollen from the stamen of one plant and transports it to the pistil of a second plant, hopefully far away.

"In order to attract bees, plants produce nectar, which the bees collect to make honey. Every time they visit a plant, some of the pollen adheres to their body. When they go to the next plant, some of the pollen comes off and germinates there. They also pick up some more pollen before they leave. The plants are able to reproduce that way, and it works fairly well.

"The problem is that there just aren't enough bees anymore. Because of pesticides, diseases, parasites, malnutrition, and human interference, bees just keep dying and disappearing. In the meantime, the demand for pollinators keeps increasing. It's a serious problem. If society can't fix it, then no amount of farming will be able to make up for the food shortage. Agriculture just won't work anymore.

"The current solution is based on breeding more bees and managing their environment more effectively. It's a difficult approach, so we aren't going to do it. Instead, we'll make fake bees.

"Because we won't be using real bees, we don't care about nectar or honey. All we want to do is get pollen from one plant to another. We're going to use nanobots – very small machines – to accomplish that."

"We're just going to make tiny robot bugs?" Jeff said.

"Basically, yes. Unlike real bugs, our nanobots are stupid. It's not that bees are particularly smart or anything, it's just that our robots will only do two things: pick up and drop off. That's it. Go to a flower and pick up. Go to another flower and drop off, then pick up. Go to another flower and drop off, then pick up, ad nauseum.

"These nanobots will be designed to pollinate, not to make honey.

101

That will make them much more efficient, and in large enough numbers, they could be incredibly helpful and cost-effective.

"The software is fairly straightforward. In the end, pollination is really just the process of moving small particles from Point A to Point B. We've been doing that with information for decades. We just program each swarm of nanobots to retrieve certain kinds of pollen and deliver them to certain plants.

"The real trick is manufacturing, because it's never been done before. Nanotechnology is in its infancy, so it will be an uphill battle. On the other hand, if we can work it out, we stand to do a lot of good and potentially make a lot of money.

"Our foundation will never be able to directly manufacture the machines, but that's not what we're here for. Our primary goal is to raise funds and stimulate further research in this area. Fortunately, I have corporate contacts who can help us get that money to the right people. Our secondary goal is to raise awareness about this problem and enable concerned people to fix it."

Karen spoke up. "So we just need to tell people about this stuff? That seems easy enough."

Kathy looked a little uncomfortable. Al turned to her.

"What's wrong?" he said. "Do you still not get it?"

"You're sitting in my chair," she said.

I cut in. "She has a bad back, Al. That chair is supposed to be for her."

Al scowled. "Well, I don't need to be here, anyway." He stood up, pulled an envelope out of his pocket, and set it on the desk. "This is a to-do list for the week. You should be able to get it all done without my assistance. I'll come in on Wednesday or Thursday to check up on your progress." He stormed out.

After a couple of seconds, he poked his head back in. "By the way, the yellow blobs are a nice touch."

Once he was gone for good, I told the employees to head home for the day, telling them we could start work on the to-do list on Tuesday morning.

I just hoped it wouldn't be more than we could handle.

Chapter Nineteen

Unlike most of the places we'd been, Johnny's Tavern was legitimately busy. Nearly all the parking spaces were full and several people were already flocking inside, but it was still early enough that we could get in without too much trouble.

Mallory parked the car and turned to me.

"They don't let people take bags inside, so that rucksack of yours will have to stay in the car. Make sure it stays out of sight."

"Will someone take it?"

"I doubt it. As often as people come in and out of here, it's not worth trying to rob the cars. Besides, nothing in there is irreplaceable."

I shoved my backpack as far under the seat as I could, and then we got out and headed toward the bar.

"What time is it?" I asked.

"It's probably another hour until nightfall," she said. "There's no way to be sure, though."

We approached the front door, and the bouncer nodded us in.

The inside of the bar was fairly subdued. I saw a small group of people on the dance floor, but none of them were putting forth any effort.

Mallory led me to an empty table near the bar.

"Here's the plan," she said. "I'll look for people I know. You look for people you know."

"I don't know that many dead people."

"Good for you. Either way, keep your eyes open."

We both looked around for a while, but I certainly didn't see anyone I knew or anyone I wanted to talk to.

Suddenly, Mallory groaned.

"Oh no, it's Satan," she said. "Don't look."

I turned to look. A pale man in a dark suit was sitting at a nearby table. His greasy black hair was arranged in an uncomfortable part, and he did seem a little sinister. Mallory hissed to get my attention, so I turned back.

"Do you think he'd be willing to help us?" I said. "Since he's in charge, he probably knows how to find Al."

Mallory laughed. "Satan isn't in charge. He just lives here."

"Seriously? Then who runs Hell?"

"The management. Anyway, Satan never helps anyone except himself. He's obnoxious." She tried to pretend that we hadn't seen him, but it was too late.

Satan stood up and casually walked over. I realized that he must have been at least 6'8", and he was almost skeletally thin.

He sat down at our table.

"Good evening, Mallory." He nodded at her. "And Douglas, it's a pleasure to meet you." He reached out to shake my hand. "I haven't seen a visitor in quite a while. If there's anything I can do to help ..."

Mallory interrupted. "We both know you aren't going to help, Satan."

Satan sneered at her. "Why don't you go get a drink, Mallory? The men are talking."

Cold fire flashed in her eyes, but she clearly knew better than to mess with the devil himself. She stood up and walked away. As soon as she was gone, Satan continued.

"As I said, Douglas, I'm here to help, so if you need anything, just say the word. Of course, an exchange would be in order."

"Do you take melted gummy bears?"

"No."

I clutched my visitor's pass. "I can't let you have this."

He chuckled. "Actually, I can leave Hell whenever I want. Despite what your companion says, I have a great deal of influence down here. My authority on Earth is a bit less, shall we say, absolute.

"I'd like for you to do me a favor when you get back there. Nothing major, just a handful of small tasks. They wouldn't take you very long."

I was skeptical. "What would I get in exchange?"

"Naturally, I'd help you find your friend Alphonse. After that, you could do whatever you want down here. I can pull a lot of strings to make this place seem just like paradise.

"Then, whenever you like, you'd just go back to Earth, take care of that business, and go about your life. Everybody wins."

"Can you be more specific about your business?"

"I'm afraid not. Nondisclosure is one of my deepest principles. I can promise that you wouldn't find any of the tasks very objectionable. In fact, they'd be quite simple."

I had read a few too many books to agree to a deal with the devil.

"Sorry, Satan, but I think I'll just take my chances for now."

He nodded. "I know. If you reconsider, just tell me." I wasn't sure how I'd find him, but I kept quiet.

He looked over his shoulder and made sure that Mallory was still sitting at the bar, staring.

"Let me give you a bit of free advice," he said. "You don't belong here. That should be patently obvious by now." He raised an eyebrow. "However, if you were to get say, 'stuck' somewhere, even that visitor's pass wouldn't be able to get you out. Then, whether you belong or not, you'd be here. Forever."

He laughed. "Of course, that's quite a longshot." His eyes narrowed. "If it did happen, I might be able to help you out." He leaned in very close. "I wouldn't ask you for a favor, though. I'd demand one."

He stood up abruptly.

"Enjoy your time here, Douglas. I think you'll find it a rather educational experience." He walked away. I had a hard time telling if he was angry or not, but I was still glad when he left the bar.

Mallory came back over, carrying a drink.

"Did he offer you something?"

"He wanted me to return to Earth and commit evil acts in exchange for helping me find Al and making Hell seem nice."

"Yeah. He's always saying stuff like that."

"You've met him before?"

"Tons of times. He gets a kick out of scheming and plotting. I don't think people ever agree to help him." She sipped her cocktail.

"What's that you're drinking?" I said.

"A Mojito. If it's going to get me hungover, I at least want it to taste good."

"A Cosmopolitan!"

She shook her head. "No, it's a Mojito. There's quite a difference."

"No, I mean, a Cosmopolitan is what Al would drink."

"Ew. Those things taste like candied fruitcake."

"I know, but how often does a man order one? Maybe the bartender remembers him."

She shrugged. "Makes sense to me. If you want to ask him, just go for it. The guy seemed pretty chatty." She kept sipping her drink.

I walked over to the bar and flagged down the bartender.

"What can I get you?" he said.

"I wanted to ask some questions."

"Fine by me." He looked around to make sure no one was waiting at the bar. "What do you want to know?"

"I just wanted to ask if any men had ordered Cosmopolitans lately."

He gave me a funny look. "I'm not running a dating service here. If you want to find a man, that's your job."

I wasn't sure what he meant, so I switched topics.

"This is your bar? Are you Johnny?"

"The one and only."

"It's neat that you get to run such a nice business. How did you come by this place?"

"Oh, that? It wasn't too hard. The only condition was that I can never leave. Ever."

"So you have to stay in this bar for the rest of eternity?"

"Exactly. I always wanted to own a bar on Earth and now I have one. It's popular these days, but if people lose interest, I'll still be here."

He shrugged. "There are places in some parts of town that don't get business anymore. Their owners are in sad shape. At least, that's what I've heard from people who can leave."

"Huh."

A scantily-dressed patron came up to the bar and Johnny went to serve her a drink. He came back a couple of minutes later.

"Anyway, if you're looking for a man, you should just introduce yourself around. A lot of these guys would be interested in a bear like you."

"I'm looking for a specific man."

"One who likes Cosmopolitans? That's a strange requirement."

"Actually, I meant a specific man named Alphonse Bloom." I described him.

Johnny nodded. "I met a guy like that a few months back. He told me that he used to be extremely rich, and I said that a lot of us were. He came in a few times but never really socialized. I think he moved away, though."

"Dang. Any idea where he went?"

"Believe it or not, I do. He overheard some people talking about computers in Suburbia and he perked up quite a bit. I'd venture a guess he ended up there eventually."

Now that two people had suggested it, I decided that Mallory and I should check out Suburbia as soon as possible.

"Thanks," I said. "You've been very helpful."

"You're welcome." He winked. "I do take tips."

"Do you mean saliva?"

He grimaced. "Not at all. Maybe something a little more useful?"

I thought about what I had on me.

"Would you like a couple of pens?"

"That could work."

I pulled two black pens out of my pocket and handed them over.

"Thanks for visiting Johnny's Tavern," he said. "Come back whenever you like."

I went back to the table, where Mallory had already finished her Mojito.

"I haven't gotten hungover in quite a while," she said. "It usually takes about eight hours to kick in."

"Was the drink any good?"

She shook her head. "Too sweet and too sour."

"Too bad. Anyway, the bartender said he'd met Al a few times. Apparently he tried to meet women but got discouraged pretty quickly. The bartender thinks he went to Suburbia because of the computers."

"So Paul was right. Good for him. I'll have to remember to thank him next time I'm in the area." She looked around. "I'm starting to worry a bit."

"There's no reason to worry. We're well on the way to finding Al."

"Not about that." She gestured to a group of men on the dance floor. "Those guys are getting kind of rowdy. I think a fight is about to break out."

I looked them over. Several of the guys were already shoving each other around.

"Do we need to leave?" I asked. "Or is this just going to settle itself?"

She shook her head. "This is going to be a big deal. See how people are reacting?"

I did. Instead of trying to avoid the scuffle, people seemed to be approaching it. Most of them were walking unsteadily and slurring their words. I couldn't hear what they were saying, but they sounded angry.

"I thought they couldn't get drunk," I said.

"They aren't drunk; they're pretending." Mallory looked on edge, too. "No matter what, don't get involved. If it gets really bad, head for the car."

"Okay, but you're coming, too, right?"

"I'll meet you there."

Across the room, the most frenetic fighter smashed his beer stein into another man's face. After that, it didn't take long for everyone else to start fighting. Oddly enough, people who weren't even near them started fighting as well. It was almost like everyone had just been waiting for something to happen.

When I realized that all the patrons were joining in, I took Mallory's advice and fled. As I moved toward the door, she pulled out her gun and ran into the fray.

For a second, I froze and watched things unfold. Other people were already pulling out weapons, from daggers to semi-automatic handguns. Several of them just used their fists, furniture, and flatware. Some of the minor brawls had already degenerated into merciless beatings.

At the bar, Johnny was standing with his arms folded, seemingly satisfied with everything. When I saw that a few patrons wanted to shift their disagreements outside, I started running.

The bouncer looked ready to start a fight of his own, but didn't seem interested in me. Most of the people in the parking lot ignored me completely, but I still felt a little nervous.

I squatted down between two cars to stay out of sight. I heard gunshots and minor explosions ringing out from the bar. A few people emerged with their fists still flying. I didn't know what to make of it, but I wanted nothing to do with any of them.

As they were fighting, the sky flashed black. Most people weren't affected, but several got dizzy and were summarily smashed. I closed my eyes and ignored the noise until it started to subside a couple of minutes later.

When I thought it was safe, I stood up and walked over to the car. It was locked, but at least I could wait for Mallory to show up.

As the noise died down, the strangest thing happened. I heard laughter. A lot of people got up, shook themselves off, and went back inside, laughing the entire time.

After a minute or so, Mallory walked out of the bar, head held high. As far as I could tell, she wasn't injured, but she wasn't laughing, either. When she got to the car, I asked her where we would stay for the night. She just shook her head.

"I won't need to sleep for another day or so," she said. "Anyway, tonight it's your turn to drive." I tried to figure out how her stamina related to my driving. "Don't worry, though, I'm going to fill up the gas tank."

I didn't understand that trade-off, either, but I decided to wait until we got farther along to ask questions.

Mallory got in the passenger side, so I had no choice but to get in behind the wheel. She handed me the keys and leaned back.

"It's your turn for this, too."

I started the car after 22 tries and we cruised off. I knew vaguely where we were going, but I double-checked with Mallory.

"Take H-15 towards H-60," she said. "We'll stop at the gas station

111

on that side of town."

"Okay." I couldn't help but ask about the fight. "What happened back there?"

"Just a fight. They happen all the time down here."

"Why?"

"Violence is all we have. Can't you tell? We go to bars to be violent. We play cards in saloons so we can start fights. We love any pretext to hurt each other, because the alternative is numbness. Eventually we get numb enough to just walk away, and that's even worse." She sighed. "And the dreams keep coming."

"I'm sorry. I didn't realize."

"I know you didn't."

"One last question: Why aren't you just constantly violent?"

"It wears us out. Besides, it hurts." She held up her left arm and I saw that her wrist was snapped backward at an impossible angle.

"This is going to take hours to go away. It might make me feel alive, but the novelty wears off."

She rubbed it a few times, and I could almost feel the popping in my own wrist.

Chapter Twenty

Al's to-do list was shorter than I expected. He wanted us to set up an official website, make some pamphlets, and set up accounts on social media sites. At the bottom, he had written, "For now, getting attention is paramount."

I admitted to Kathy, Karen, and Jeff that I didn't know much about website design.

"I was more of a theoretical computer scientist," I said. "Websites were a bit too practical for me."

"My son is a whiz at that," Kathy said. "He made home pages for all of our family pets."

"Do you think he'd be willing to take on some freelance work?"

"Definitely. He's always looking for something to do."

"Good! When can he come by?"

"Probably after 3:00 today. That's when he gets off."

"Okay. That settles that. So who here knows how to use all the social media sites? I don't use any myself."

"Too practical?" Jeff said.

"No, just too social," I said. "Do you know anything about them?"

"Yeah, I have accounts on all the big ones."

"Okay. Get started on that. I'll send you our logo. Al emailed it to me several times." I turned to Karen. "You're good at interior design stuff. Could you apply that knowledge to create pamphlets somehow?"

"Sure," she said. "What should they say?"

"Oh, something about pollination and bees. Just look up some information online."

"Can do."

"Great. In the meantime, I'll see if any local papers might be interested in our project. Maybe they'll want to come down and see the office or something."

We all went to our desks and started working. Kathy called her son and left a message, then starting playing games online. I assumed she could keep an eye out for any visitors while Jeff was joining sites and creating profiles.

Throughout the day, we kept thinking of things we hadn't bought, so I made a couple of trips to buy supplies. The bathroom was shared among all the offices on our floor, so everyone had to make an occasional trip there as well.

We had no way to prepare or store lunches, so I put "microwave" and "refrigerator" on a list of larger purchases I needed to make. We wouldn't be able to get plumbing in the office, so I also added "water cooler" to the list.

I managed to get ahold of the Akron Beacon Journal and invited them to check out the project's office. I outlined our basic objectives to the receptionist, who explained that they had higher priorities but might come by in the next few days.

When I called the local news station, they just hung up on me.

Around 3:15, Kathy's son showed up. It had never occurred to me that he might only be nine years old.

"Hey, sweetie," she said. "Doug, this is my son, Seth."

"Is that right?" I flashed a fake smile. "I hear you're quite the web designer."

"I guess so," Seth said. "I really just goof around, though."

"Oh, don't be modest," she said. "Show him the page you made for little Kodiak."

The boy shrugged, went to her computer, and loaded "www.iheartkodiak.com." The website comprised several images of a brown wiener dog in various silly outfits. The design was amateurish and the code was clearly incorrect in several parts.

I felt like our website should be better maintained, so I tried to think of the best way to explain it to Seth.

"We need a more boring site," I said. "This one is just too exciting. Ours has to appeal to rich, old grown-ups."

"Okay." Seth shrugged. "I really didn't want to do it, anyway." I sighed in relief, then I looked over at Kathy, who was trying not to cry.

"I'm just so proud of you," she said, embracing Seth. "I don't want this to hold back your career."

"Mom, it's fine."

"I need to take the rest of the afternoon off," she sobbed.

Kathy grabbed Seth and rushed out of the room before I could say anything. I stared after them.

Jeff spoke up. "I got us accounts on Facebook, Tumblr, LinkedIn, and Twitter."

"That's excellent news." I walked over to his desk. "Show me what you have so far."

He opened up several browser windows and loaded the web pages. The image of Brad was perfect, but Jeff had misspelled "Pollinator" as "Pollenater" on all the accounts.

"That isn't how you spell 'pollinator,'" I said.

"Really? How is it spelled?"

"The same way as in the logo."

"Oh. That makes sense."

"I think so, too. Can you fix it?"

"Yes, but I'll have to open new accounts. You can't change your account name without deleting the whole thing."

115

I sighed. "Okay. Go ahead and do that."

I walked over to Karen's desk, where she was printing off pamphlets and folding them together.

"These look nice," I said.

"Thanks," she said. "I spent all day on them." I picked up a few to put on the reception desk. I was about to read one when I heard the front door open.

To my surprise, two visitors entered: a man wearing a beige trench coat and a small woman with a large camera. I walked over to introduce myself.

"We're from the Akron Beacon Journal," the reporter said. "It was a slow news day, so we came to check out your operation."

"Excellent! I'm Doug DeWitt, the Chief Executive Officer." I gestured to the rest of the room. "This is the office." I pointed to Jeff. "That's Jeff."

"Fascinating. So what exactly do you do here, Doug?"

"We raise awareness about issues relating to pollinator decline. We're also funding research to produce an artificial pollinator using nanotechnology. Let me give you some literature about the project."

I handed him one of Karen's pamphlets and took the opportunity to look one over myself. It contained several key facts such as "bees are insects" and "honey is made from nectar," but I didn't see any information about our charity or goals. It read more like a third-grade report on honeybees.

"According to this pamphlet," the reporter said, "pollination is just plant sex." He looked up. "Should I run that in the article?"

I blushed. "I'd rather you didn't. Maybe you could just mention the nanotechnology."

Suddenly, the photographer took my picture. I wasn't prepared for the flash, so I flinched.

The reporter continued. "Well, this pamphlet is certainly helpful." He pocketed it. "Do you have anything else you want to share with the paper?"

"Our website isn't up yet, but we do have a social media presence."

"I see. Can you give me the link?"

"It's not quite ready. I can show you basically what it should look like." I walked over to Jeff's desk and pointed to the Facebook page. "We'll get a newer version up in the next couple of days."

"I do like that bee." He turned to the photographer. "What do you think?" She nodded, and then he turned back to me.

"Well, Doug, I think we have everything we need for a really good article."

He shook my hand again and left without saying anything else. The photographer waved goodbye on the way out. All told, their visit took about three minutes. I had a hard time believing the article would be any good at all.

The employees and I went home for the day. I was feeling particularly dejected, so I just went to bed when I got home and slept for about 13 hours.

I woke up at 8:00, showered, and drove back to work. I arrived before everyone else, so I opened everything up.

When the employees arrived, they all looked a bit grim. Jeff was holding a copy of the morning newspaper.

"You might want to check this out," he said.

I took the paper and skimmed through it. Fortunately, the article, "The Pollenater [sic] Project Kicks Off," didn't make the front page.

On the other hand, it didn't reflect well on us. The text was mostly about our limited knowledge of honeybees and our incompetent yet well-meaning staff.

As for the graphic, they used the candid photo of me instead of our logo. I looked vaguely scared and constipated.

I told the employees to get back to work. Jeff needed to set up the new social media accounts and Kathy was supposed to look around

117

for a web design artist. She seemed resigned to the fact that her son wouldn't be able to help. Karen had to get more information for the pamphlet and check with me before printing anything off.

Al called around lunchtime.

"When I told you that attention was paramount," he said, "I meant positive attention. I didn't want our environmental organization to look more birdbrained than the Audubon Society."

"That article was a fluke," I said. "They showed up before we were ready."

"Obviously. Look, just fix your mistakes, and I'll see if I can get us on the local news tomorrow. Maybe if we can show that we worked the kinks out, we won't be the laughingstock of the non-profit community.

"In the meantime, I've got a couple other things in the works, so I'm leaving this to you."

"Okay. I promise it won't be problem."

"Good. If I'm going to attract women, it won't be with the world's silliest non-profit. On that note, make sure the cameras get a good shot of Brad the Beedroid. I definitely don't want your face representing this project." I agreed, then he hung up.

After that, I decided to take a more active role and verified everyone's progress toward their respective goals. If nothing else, I needed to make sure I wouldn't take the blame for any future mistakes.

Chapter Twenty-One

I was surprised to find that Hell's freeways were almost empty at night. I still had to avoid the stalled cars and construction zones, but it wasn't too bad apart from that.

The missing headlight was a bit more troublesome. We had reattached the left headlight after it fell off, but it no longer worked, so our car stayed cycloptic. There were enough lights in the city that it wouldn't be an issue, but in the rest of Hell, we'd have a hard time with visibility.

Mallory insisted that we continue traveling, even though it was clear that she really just wanted to avoid sleep at all costs. She directed me to a gas station on the edge of the city.

The building itself was a nondescript little shop with a sign on top that said "Gas." There were four pumps, all vacant.

I pulled in next to one of them, only to discover that the gas tank was on the other side of the car and the hose was too short. I had to get back in, find the right key, start the car, and move it into the correct position. Mallory glared at me the entire time.

When I finally got the car lined up correctly, I asked the obvious question: "How do we pay for the gasoline? There aren't any price signs around."

"Gas isn't too expensive," Mallory said. "You only have to drink one cup of gasoline for every gallon you put in the car." I must have looked surprised, because she added, "I told you I'd do it, remember?"

"Thanks." I didn't exactly understand how the process worked, so I just had to watch and see. Mallory went inside the building and spoke with the clerk, then she came back out with an extremely large styrofoam drink cup.

On the side, it read "The Urinator." I thought the name was strange given the fact that no one in Hell urinated.

She got back in the car. "This is a half-gallon, so that gives us eight gallons in the car. As soon as I finish, the pump will start working."

"Why do they call it The Urinator?" I asked.

"They use these cups for water, too. If you drink the water, it makes you feel like you're about to piss yourself, except you can't. It goes away after a couple of hours."

"Huh."

"Yeah. Fortunately, the gas doesn't do that. Now shut up and let me drink this." She put the straw in her mouth and started drinking, but gagged after a couple of gulps.

"I'll get it, it just takes some time." She breathed deeply for a second or two.

I thought of something. "Wait a second. Let me see that cup."

"Gladly." She handed the cup over, and I examined it.

"This cup is definitely styrofoam, but that doesn't make any sense. The gasoline should have melted it."

"What do you mean?"

"I mean that styrofoam dissolves in gasoline. Believe me, I've seen it."

"So what? That isn't gas?"

I opened it up and sniffed it. "It doesn't smell like gas to me."

"What?" She grabbed it back and smelled for herself. "You're right, it doesn't. But a second ago ..." She sipped it again. "It's just water. I don't even have to pee or anything."

She stared at me. "I've choked down hundreds of gallons of this.

120

You're telling me it only tasted like gas because I thought it would?"

I shrugged. "I guess. I honestly don't know."

"Thank you." She looked genuinely grateful.

"You're very welcome."

"Let's share." We drank the rest of the "gas" together, then she got out and filled the tank. When she got back in, she was all business.

"Now we can head out. We'll take H-60 out of The Big City toward Suburbia."

"Suburbia must be fairly close to The Big City, right?"

"You'd think that, but no. It's actually a good distance away."

"Are you sure you can't drive? I have no idea how to get there."

"I'll give you directions, so don't worry. Besides, I've been drinking." She paused. "I might not be drunk, but I'll have a Hell of a hangover in a few hours."

"From one cocktail?"

"Yeah." I dropped the subject and got back on the freeway. Exiting The Big City was much easier than entering. I just had to follow the freeway until it ended abruptly.

After that, we resumed our bumpy journey along the telephone pole path. Despite Mallory's assertions, she looked tired. I was starting to get a little sleepy myself. I decided to spark up another conversation.

"Can you tell any funny stories?" I said.

She glared at me. "I don't really do funny."

"I never got to finish the one from before, so I thought maybe—"

"No! Let's see." She thought for a second. "Okay, one time Cody and I were high – not any anything major, just pot. Anyway, we decided to bake a cake, but neither one of us knew how to do it.

"Cody said we obviously needed to start with a cake, so we went to the local grocery store and bought the nicest cake we could find."

"You mean a finished cake?"

"Yeah. It was frosted and decorated with some birthday message.

As soon as we got home, we turned the oven up to 500 degrees and put it in, plastic container and everything."

"Gross."

"You don't know the half of it. Naturally, the container melted and the cake burned, but we fell asleep before we noticed anything. When I woke up, I ran in and turned the oven off, but it was way too late.

"The entire house was full of thick, black smoke, and the kitchen was stained with soot and residue. It stank like you wouldn't believe. Fortunately, there wasn't much damage to the rest of the house.

"We thought about buying a new oven, but it would have eaten into our drug budget. We decided to buy a five-dollar toaster oven at a yard sale. For the rest of our lease, the kitchen was useless; we lived off of grilled cheese sandwiches and the occasional toasted hot dog.

"When we moved out a couple of months later, the landlady had a fit. She tried to charge us for the damages, but we flaked out. In that sense, it had a happy ending. Funny enough for you?"

"Sort of. It was a little bleaker than I expected."

"Well, I warned you," she said.

"Maybe we should just stop and sleep for a little while?"

"No. We'll get robbed or something."

I looked at our barren surroundings.

"That doesn't seem likely."

"Just shut up and drive."

"Okay." I thought back to Driver's Ed. "You know, I still remember the three rules of drowsy driving: stay cold and keep your eyes moving. See, if your body is cold, you're less likely to get comfortable and fall asleep. Plus if you don't fix your gaze on a specific point, your brain won't be able to relax. You're much less likely to fall asleep that way."

"What's the third rule?"

"Oh, right. The third rule of drowsy driving is 'don't do it.' It's way too dangerous."

Mallory sighed and stared out the window. I clearly wasn't supposed to mess with her now. It occurred to me that the jalopy had no air conditioning, so the car was extremely warm, and the horizon was the same in every direction, so moving my eyes didn't help anything. I was breaking all the rules, but I still did what I could to stay awake.

After a few minutes, I looked over and saw that Mallory had fallen asleep. I doubted that she wanted to keep sleeping, so I reached out my arm to wake her up.

When I leaned over, my hand slipped off the steering wheel and the car started jostling a little too much. Before I could shake her, I had to grab the wheel again.

The car was vibrating wildly to the right, so I panicked and swerved to the left, ramming the jalopy directly into a telephone pole.

At 15 miles per hour, I doubted it did much damage. Instead of checking things out, I just leaned back and went to sleep.

Chapter Twenty-Two

The Pollinator Project's television appearance worked out surprisingly well. Karen and I put together an informational pamphlet, Kathy hired a designer to throw together a rudimentary website, and Jeff got all our social media accounts set up correctly.

We planned on fleshing things out later, but at least our organization would seem legitimate on TV.

Al had warned us that the reporters would arrive in the afternoon. Naturally, he wanted to make an appearance, so he showed up about 30 minutes early, wearing a tuxedo.

I was just wearing jeans and a T-shirt.

"Don't you think you're a little underdressed?" he said.

"For the six o'clock news?" I said.

Al frowned. "Even so. You have that one collared shirt, right? The one you wore to Cleveland?"

"I haven't done laundry since then."

He sighed. "Well, at least I'll look better by comparison."

The employees were wearing business casual attire, so I did look the least composed. On the other hand, I was the CEO. I didn't have to impress anyone.

Al looked over our various projects and nodded his approval.

"I think we'll be able to make a good presentation. None of you should talk unless I instruct you to." He turned to me. "That includes you, Didi. By the way, don't stand next to me. You make me look short."

"Noted." I sighed.

The TV people came in and Al greeted them with fanfare. The reporter was a prominent female correspondent from Channel 4. I couldn't remember her name, but Al called her Cindy. I was pretty sure he was wrong, but she didn't correct him.

Cindy was dressed conservatively but took an active interest in Al. The cameraman followed her inside. He kept the camera pointed at her, ate a sub sandwich, and ignored everyone else.

Cindy explained that their goal was to get footage of the office space, including shots of the employees working, and to do an interview with Al and me. The footage would be spliced together for the evening broadcast.

She suggested that we start with the establishing shots, so the other employees and I went to our desks and pretended to work. Jeff wrote random words on a notepad, Kathy and Karen typed, and I pretended to talk on the phone.

"It doesn't matter what you say," Cindy told me. "I'll be talking over this part." I recited some mathematical theorems and eventually hung up on myself. After that, Cindy took Al aside and interviewed him.

At the very end of the visit, she asked me two questions: "What do you do here?" and "Where's the bathroom?"

I explained that I was the CEO in charge of day-to-day operations and that the bathroom was down the hallway. She and the camera guy left immediately. He still hadn't finished his sandwich.

Al waved goodbye and walked through the office, congratulating everyone on a job well pretended. Before he left, Al mentioned that a fellow scientist would be coming by in a couple of days.

"The guy's name is Professor Harold Matheson; he's a computational entomologist. Apparently he's familiar with swarm intelligence and pollination, so I shot him an email outlining our plans. He should be willing to help. I told him to just visit the office on Friday, so be ready."

Al headed out the door, whistling.

Afterwards, I told the employees to be ready to field phone calls and emails the next day, due to the attention from our TV appearance.

I let everyone leave early so we'd have plenty of time to get home and watch the news. I got home at 5:30 and turned on the television while I prepared and ate a frozen TV dinner.

Most of the news was routine stuff. Our segment was scheduled for the human interest slot at the very end, which meant I had to wait until 6:26. On the segment itself, the reporter said her name was Cynthia Jensen, so that explained the name discrepancy.

Most of the segment was focused on Al, who spoke about the amount of money he had and how it was going to be spent, placing significantly more emphasis on himself than on the project.

My sole interview question didn't make the final cut, but my imaginary telephone conversation did.

The next morning, we got surprisingly few phone calls or emails. In fact, no one called at all until around 11:15. Naturally, it was Al.

"Didi, you'll never guess who called me last night!" he said.

"Please don't make me do this," I said.

"It was Tina! You know, Dr. Cherry? She saw me on TV and called to tell me I look great in a tuxedo. I had no idea she lived around here! Did you know?"

"No," I lied.

"I didn't think so. Anyway, I just wanted to give you a heads-up. I'm going to go visit her for the next few days, so I'll be incommunicado until next week."

"What about this entomologist? He might want to talk with you about the project."

"I sent you a work-up. Just write down all his concerns and save

126

them for next week, okay? This is more important."

I disagreed, but as always, Al would get his way.

I was going to ask what had happened with Dr. Cherry the last time but he hung up before I could say anything.

Chapter Twenty-Three

I woke up under a somewhat bright gray sky. Now that I had driven at night, I appreciated the daytime much more.

The car was still rammed against the pole, and Mallory was still asleep. I knew she'd want me to wake her up, but I wasn't sure how to do it without getting bruised.

I decided to use my backpack as a sort of shield and pushed it against her.

She screamed herself awake, but didn't punch anything this time. As soon as she stopped screaming, she grabbed her forehead and moaned.

"What was I thinking?" She took several deep breaths. "I hate Mojitos."

She was clearly hurting from the hangover, so I stayed silent. After a second or two, she looked around.

"Where the Hell are we?" She turned to me. "Did you run into a pole?"

"I'm not going to lie," I said. "Yes."

She looked angry for a second, then relaxed. "Well, we both fell asleep. How long did you drive after I passed out?"

"At least three or four minutes."

She rolled her eyes. "Excellent. Let's check out the damage."

We got out and examined the front of the car.

"This thing is dented," I said. "What's it called?"

"That's the hood, Doug."

"It doesn't have a special name or anything?"

"No." She knelt down and looked underneath the car. "We shook loose a ton of parts. There's no way this thing's going to start up again."

"We could try."

"You can try, if you want. I bet all the keys will get you the same response, though: nothing."

I checked under the car and realized she was right. Most of the jalopy seemed to have fallen off. We both stood up.

"What do we do now?" I said.

"Isn't it obvious? We walk. Grab your rucksack and let's go." I got my backpack out of the car and looked around for anything else of value.

Mallory threw the key ring in the car and said, "Good riddance."

I looked at the front of the car one last time. The pole was so sturdy it hadn't moved at all.

"These really are well-maintained," I said.

We started our trek anew. After a few minutes, I had to ask the obvious question: "How much farther is it to Suburbia?"

"I honestly can't remember. It's close to the outskirts."

"Outskirts? I thought Hell went on forever."

"It does, but once you get a certain distance away from the center, you have a harder time getting back. The damned only go past that boundary if they're sure they want to completely isolate themselves."

"I see. So the farther out you go, the more you get pulled out. It's sort of like hyperbolic geometry. The disk model."

"If you say so."

"Have you ever gone past the border?"

"No. It's a lot more fun to stick near the center with all the newly damned souls. They say everyone moves away eventually, though. I don't know if it's true."

"Do you see yourself doing it?"

"Not anytime soon." She got a strange look on her face but I couldn't tell why.

We walked together for another hour or so until I saw something that broke the monotony: a huge field of skullflowers scattered around the next few telephone poles.

"I hate this part," Mallory said.

I was amazed at the sheer size of the field. "Where did all these flowers come from?"

"When people drive Hummers from The Big City to Suburbia, they run out of gas around here," she said. "It happens a lot."

When we got closer, I could see the remains of several SUVs that had run out of gas. I assumed the flowers were the remains of the drivers.

"Don't talk to any of these things," Mallory said. "They'll just suck you into lame conversations."

"Okay. Maybe we can use one of their cars, though."

"Don't bet on it. As soon as the drivers abandon them, they start sinking into the ground." She was right. All the nearby Hummers were half-submerged in the gray dirt. I could tell that they hadn't been around very long.

The skullflowers were all whistling. Some of them were trying to carry a tune, the rest were improvising. They stared at us, twisting their blue stems in unison as we went by.

None of them spoke, but Mallory still gave them a wide berth. I decided to wave, but other than that, I ignored them, too.

After we passed the field completely, I had to ask Mallory a question.

"What do you have against skullflowers? The ones I've seen are pleasant enough."

"They're weak. As soon as something doesn't go their way, they just lie down and give up. It's the easy way out."

"They're stuck in the ground forever. What's easy about that?"

Mallory started to get red in the face. "Those little daisies have nothing to worry about. They just sit around and rest, never thinking or doing anything. Their heads are completely empty; the skulls are the only thing left. They can't even remember their names!"

She turned around and glared at me.

"That's never going to happen to me!"

I backed up a bit. "I never said it would."

"Good. Don't forget it." She turned back and started moving even faster.

We walked for quite a while. I was pleased to find that I didn't get tired physically, just mentally. On the other hand, I was almost more discouraged by the fact that I could walk for days without wearing out.

To kill some time, I started factoring integers in numerical order. I had just determined that 353 was prime when Mallory got bored enough to start talking again.

"It might be hard to believe," she said, "but I've occasionally made some friends down here. Former drug addicts, dealers, adulterers. My people, I guess. In the end, they always just gave up. Now they're all in places like that field.

"I visited one of them once, just to see what she had to say. She couldn't remember who she was and didn't recognize me. I tried explaining our friendship together but she just kept talking about the weather. When I mentioned that there was no such thing as weather down here, she got very angry and refused to talk.

"Finally, I just buried her. She clearly had no interest in existing and I didn't want to see her like that anymore."

"Did she come back up?"

"Probably. I never checked." She paused. "That's enough about me. Tell me why you're visiting your nemesis. I need to know why

131

we're going through all this."

"You're right, you deserve to know. I'm just not sure where to begin." I sighed. "To start with, I need his help."

Chapter Twenty-Four

The Pollinator Project got phone calls for several days after the TV segment. No one wanted to donate, but we were able to give them rudimentary information and direct them to our website and Facebook page.

I kept organizing things, and the staff was starting to work well together. We had worked out the chore schedule and the fridge had shown up, so everyone was pretty happy.

What surprised me the most was how much fun it was. Instead of trying to patch together a flawed organization using archaic methods, I got to start from scratch. Other people had to negotiate with me.

We hadn't spent much of Al's money yet, and I thought he'd be pleased. I still needed to pay myself and the workers, but Karen told me that there were special rules about paychecks.

She said we had to go through a payroll service provider to get proper paychecks, tax withholding, and so on. It sounded complicated.

Karen called the people she knew and started the process, but we'd have to wait another week or so for everything to get completely set up.

Professor Matheson hadn't visited yet, but I had planned some questions for our meeting. Al had emailed me his "work-up" before he left. The information was pretty complicated, but I was able to follow everything, for the most part.

Apparently Al had a good method for structuring the swarm and communicating with the nanobots, but he didn't understand the specifics of pollination. He needed the entomologist to explain different methods of detecting pollen.

The more Al understood the process, the better he'd be able to design our detection mechanism. I also noticed one offhand footnote about construction materials, but it never came up again, so I ignored it.

Professor Matheson arrived first thing on Friday morning. For some reason, I expected a friend of Al's to be irresponsible. This one meant business. Like many academics, he was dressed casually but walked stiffly.

I greeted him at the door.

"You must be Professor Matheson," I said.

His eyes narrowed. "Call me Harry. I insist."

"Okay." We stared at each other for a moment. "I'm Doug."

"I know who you are, Mr. DeWitt. I'm here to talk business."

The conversation was a bit more adversarial than I expected. I tried to figure out how to proceed.

"Do you want, um, lunch or something?"

He checked his watch. "It's 9:15 a.m. We can talk over brunch."

He turned and walked out. I was clearly supposed to follow him, so I waved goodbye to the other employees and left. Hopefully they could run the place without me.

Harry walked so briskly to the nearby coffee shop that I had a hard time keeping up. He went in and ordered, then faced me and crossed his arms. I ordered a hot chocolate and paid for his espresso and three scones.

Harry sat down in a booth by the window. I joined him, still a little confused by his demeanor.

"Dr. Bloom told me that you need my assistance," he said. "I think I can provide it. I'm perfectly willing to write you a comprehensive paper on this subject. It should give you everything you need."

"That's excellent news."

He held up his index finger. "I didn't say I'd provide it for free. Dr. Bloom offered me two million dollars."

I blinked. "Why did he do that?"

Harry laughed. "He knows I'm the foremost expert on pollination, of course. The process isn't as simple as Dr. Bloom seems to think. Beyond honeybees, there are thousands of other vectors responsible for pollinating a wide variety of plants. Some methods are quite ornate and specific to certain species.

"I'll give you everything I know, but I want what's coming to me." He raised an eyebrow. "In advance."

"Well, Professor—"

"Harry!"

"Yes, Harry, this is a large undertaking. I know your advice will be helpful, but I can't pay you that amount, certainly not in advance."

"In that case, I'm walking." Harry stood and picked up his scones. "I insist that you reimburse my airfare. I flew here from Calgary on good faith."

"Canada?" Al must have been more serious than I thought. I worried what he would say, so I caved in. "Fine! We'll pay you the two million. I promise. If it's important to Al, it's important to me."

"I thought so." He sat back down.

"The thing is, I'm not authorized to pay you that much." I took out the checkbook. "I can give you $49,000 right now, but that's all."

"That will do for now. American dollars, of course."

"Of course." I wrote the check out to Professor Harold Matheson. I had never even seen a check for that much money, let alone written one. I handed it over to him.

"We, um, look forward to working with you."

"I know." He examined the check. "This bee is cute, but biologically inaccurate in several ways. I certainly hope your artificial

135

pollinators are better constructed.

"In any case, I'm flying back to Calgary tomorrow. I'll cash this check when I get there, but I want to speak with Alphonse himself before I start work in earnest."

"I understand. He should be available early next week."

"Very well." Harry gathered up his scones and coffee and walked out.

I drank my hot chocolate for a few minutes and tried not to think about the amount of money I had just promised to spend.

I returned to the office and went through my routine for the day. I was glad when I finished so I could at least relax for the weekend.

After everyone else left, I decided to call Al and leave a message on his cell phone. To my surprise, he picked up after a few rings.

"Hey, Didi. I thought I said I was incommunicado."

"You did. I was just going to leave a message."

"Well, now you don't have to. What's up?"

"I spoke with Professor Matheson this morning."

"You mean Harry?

"I do. He said he'd write us a comprehensive paper, but only if we pay him in advance."

"That seems fair."

"Good. I gave the guy a check for $49,000 today to placate him, but I promised to pay him two million dollars, just like you offered."

There was a long pause. "Doug, I only offered him 200 grand."

"What!? He said two million, I swear!" I started to sweat.

"Imagine that. Did you try to negotiate?"

I stuttered for a second. "But I thought ... he said that you ..."

"It's okay, Didi. Those sensors are the most critical part of our machines. Anyway, computational entomologists have a reputation for driving hard bargains."

"Among who?"

"Themselves, mostly. Anyway, this stuff is important enough to

136

warrant the expense, but you should use more discretion in the future. It's my money you're spending, not yours."

"I know. I'm sorry."

"Don't apologize." He hung up without saying anything else.

I found myself wishing he'd use some kind of valediction once in a while.

Chapter Twenty-Five

"I know I've mentioned this before," I said, "but Al is brilliant. He has the potential to revolutionize any number of industries or branches of science. At least, he used to have the potential."

"Then he killed himself." Mallory said.

"Exactly. See, a few of his early inventions made him tens of millions of dollars. He was so rich he didn't even care where his money went, or at least that's what I thought.

"One day, he decided he wanted to do some good in the world." I paused. "Actually, he did it to get women interested in him."

"Why didn't he just pay for sex?"

"I wondered that, too. Apparently he wanted a true relationship, not just prostitution. He set aside 20 million dollars for a charity called the Pollinator Project, and I was in charge of running it.

"Our goal was to design a way of pollinating crops that circumvented pollinator decline. If we succeeded, we stood a chance of reducing hunger and food shortages everywhere."

"Huh. Sounds impressive."

"It was. The project lasted less than three weeks before Al and his money abandoned us."

"Easy come, easy go. So when did he kill himself?"

"I'm getting to that part." I sighed. "You're even more impatient than I am. Anyway, there was this woman, Dr. Celestina Cherry."

She snorted. "That has to be a fake name."

"What makes you so sure?"

"Nobody names their daughter Celestina Cherry."

"Cherry might not have been her maiden name, though."

She chuckled. "It better have been."

I sighed. "May I continue?"

"Please."

"Anyway, Tina was Al's kryptonite. Whenever she showed up, everything went straight to Hell. I have no idea why. She convinced him to start working on another project, so he put his money into that instead."

"Something nerdy?"

"Of course. He also stood to make more money with the new project. He moved in with Tina and their relationship started getting really serious. After about six months, he proposed. She told him no, then broke up with him out of the clear blue sky."

"Why?"

"I never found out. Shortly after that, he shot himself."

"Damn. She must have said some pretty serious stuff. You really don't know what happened?"

"I really don't. As for me, I kept working on the Pollinator Project in my spare time. Through sheer determination and stubbornness, I scraped together some funds to revive the project, but just barely.

"I got together all the information that Al had needed, then I started looking for someone to replace him."

I shook my head. "It was impossible. He was leaps and bounds above everyone else in the field. The foremost computer scientist I could find said the technology was at least ten years away, maybe even twenty. Al seemed to think he could do it within two. I believed him."

"So you need him to do the stuff he was supposed to do in the first place?"

"Right. I arranged to get a visitor's pass to Hell so I could discuss

139

it with him. When I find Al, I'm going to have him outline everything as clearly as possible, then I'll take the information back to Earth and get the project restarted for real.

"If I can get enough information, hopefully other scientists will pick up on Al's ideas. We should be able to do a lot of good. His help is invaluable. I don't know what I'd do without him," I said. "Literally."

"Yeah, that's a neat idea. Too bad he won't do it."

"Of course he will." I stopped walking. "Why wouldn't he?"

Mallory turned back to look at me. "Why should he help you? He's dead. No one wants to make a better world they're never going back to."

"Yes, but—"

"And he refused to help you on Earth, didn't he? It's clearly not that important to him."

She kept walking. "Don't take my word for it, though. Let him tell you himself."

I didn't buy into her cynicism, but I did start to worry. What if I made it all this way and Al still refused to help?

Mallory was gaining ground, so I started walking again to catch up with her. I hoped we'd get to Suburbia soon.

Chapter Twenty-Six

I spent the weekend watching TV and trying not to think about money. I started to get a good picture of how the Pollinator Project would work. Al seemed to have his plan almost squared away, but I still didn't know how the manufacturing would proceed.

Presumably, our office would facilitate the process, acting as a liaison between all the different parties. The fact that we were providing the money meant we got to negotiate.

Within a couple of years, we might have even had a viable prototype. The project would spark a revolutionary approach to agriculture. My optimism knew no bounds. Best of all, I finally felt like I was doing something meaningful instead of just spinning my proverbial wheels.

On Monday morning, I showed up a bit early. It was hard to believe the project was already in its third week. I felt like we had gotten a lot accomplished so far.

When I arrived at the office door, I saw that someone was already inside. I knew I had locked it on Friday, and Al was the only other person with a key. Hopefully, he'd be willing to talk business.

I went inside and found Al sitting in Kathy's chair, whistling cheerily.

"Good morning, Didi," he said. "It's a beautiful Monday."

I shrugged. "I guess. What's up with you?"

"I spent an excellent weekend in Cleveland with Tina. It was one of the nicest times I think I've ever had."

"It seems so. I meant, did you make any progress with the project?"

"Nah. I was busy." He gave me a sly wink. "Besides, I had to wait for that bug guy's report. Tina said 'Hi,' by the way."

"Hi to Tina." I thought for a second. "Whatever happened between you two? I thought you guys broke up back in North Carolina."

"Oh, that. Well, she was always a little clingy. The first time around, I wasn't ready for that all. I mean, I was a college freshman. I didn't think long-term."

"That's strange. You were so excited about her at the beginning. I mean, you slept with her out of nowhere."

He shook his head. "Like I told everyone, I went to her office to talk about atheism. Tina practically threw herself at me. Seriously."

He frowned. "She wouldn't take no for an answer. It was actually kind of scary."

His smile returned. "Anyway, we rendezvoused again senior year. She was sad at Christmas, so I took her to that one party. I can barely remember it, but it rebooted our relationship.

"After the spring semester, she wanted to follow me all the way to Paris, but I said no. She started talking about fidelity and stuff like that, but I still shot her down. I had my priorities straight."

He winked again. "Now that she's here, I realized I what a good thing I had going back then. We got back together and this time, it's for real. On that note, I wanted to talk to you about something."

Before he could continue, Kathy walked in. I could see that she was annoyed about Al sitting in her chair.

"Hello, Karen," he said.

"I'm Kathy."

"That's what I meant."

She walked directly over to the chair and hovered over him. Al

142

stared at her for a few seconds, the turned back to me.

"Look, I'll just call you later tonight."

He stood up and walked out, completely ignoring Kathy, who sat down and sighed.

"There's nothing like good lumbar support," she said. I was worried about what Al wanted to tell me, but I'd have to wait.

Later that afternoon, the office got a call from Professor Matheson. Jeff handed me the phone and I took it over to my phone call corner.

"Good afternoon, Harry," I said. "I trust you made it back to Calgary without incident?"

"Cut the crap, DeWitt. Your check bounced."

I froze. "That's impossible."

"The Hell it is. We had an agreement and you wrote me a bad check. You can kiss my help goodbye." He hung up.

I turned to Jeff. "He just hung up without saying anything. What happened to courtesy?"

"I have no idea," Jeff said. "I always say something before I hang up."

"Good for you." All afternoon and evening, I kept wondering how I would break the news to Al. He finally called me around 8:00.

"Didi!" he said. "I wanted to tell you this morning, but I have the best news! Apparently, Tina knows a guy in the video game industry who's interested in creating better A.I. for his company's games."

"Okay, but what does that have to do with our project?"

"Well, it's better than your project. First of all, it'll make money. Second of all, it combines artificial and biological neural networks.

"We're going to grow miniature brains in jars and connect them to video game consoles with a brand-new interface, developed by yours truly. We'll be able to reproduce humanlike intelligence in completely artificial video game players!"

"In other words, you're going to make fake video gamers so that real video gamers will face more of a challenge?"

143

"Exactly! No one plays video games better than humans. Anyway, we stand to make a huge profit, so I redirected the pollen fund into a non-profit organization for this. The pollen stuff was getting expensive. After all, two million was a little steep for that guy's paper. I have no idea why you promised him that much."

"But I didn't—" I stopped and thought for a second. "Wait, how is this non-profit if your main focus is earning money?"

"We're sponsored by another non-profit organization, the National Football League."

"Right, but what about the Pollinator Project?"

"What do you mean? It's over. I'm moving on." I tried to think of something to say, but came up short. "Look, Tina's waving at me to get off the phone. I'll talk to you later." He hung up abruptly, but at least he had said goodbye for once.

Chapter Twenty-Seven

Mallory and I walked until nightfall without speaking again. It was like we were in two different worlds. I had no idea what she was thinking, but I was contemplating eternity.

I couldn't truly appreciate that Hell lasted forever and extended infinitely in every direction. In Hell, people threw around words like "forever" and "infinite" without even blinking, but in reality, the ideas were overwhelming.

I never understood it in math, either. They said that there were countably infinite sets, things you could count out and never stop: 1, 2, 3, 4, and so on. Then there were the uncountably infinite sets, which were even bigger than "normal" infinity.

They said that there were as many "real" numbers between 1 and 2 as there were above 2. How could that be real? Then they had the audacity to say that some numbers were even more infinite.

In the true real world, nothing was infinite. The universe was bounded. Time was bounded. Even boundless human imagination had its bounds. How could a place exist without any bounds? If it did, what could anyone do in a hundred-year life span to deserve living there? I was surrounded by people whose mistakes had cost them absolutely everything.

I wondered what kind of people ran the place. "The management" sounded awfully vague, but no one seemed to know anything else.

When the sky flashed black, I didn't even flinch.

"Should we rest?" I said.

"Are you tired?"

"Nope. How about you?"

"No. I think we'll get there around dawn at this rate. Let's just keep going."

We walked on into the darkness. After a while, I was asleep on my feet, moving automatically without even paying. It was hard to see in the dark, but my flashlight was inoperable.

In the middle of the night, I got out a stale peanut butter sandwich and ate it to break the monotony. The flavor was about right, but the texture was like eating a paste-filled pumice stone. I chased it down with a bottle of water and went back to trudging along.

The telephone poles never stopped coming. The landscape never changed. Even the random spurts of flame had stopped.

When the sky flashed gray again. I realized we had just spent an entire 24 hours walking, maybe even 26, given the strange day lengths. We had probably covered at least a hundred miles. I could never have done that on Earth.

Then again, I wouldn't have wanted to.

"That's Suburbia," Mallory said, pointing to the horizon. "Do you see it?"

I peered into the distance but couldn't see anything out of the ordinary.

"Not really."

"It's just a smudge right now. It'll stand out more when we get closer."

As we approached, I noticed that the horizon was taking on a reddish tinge, but only on the left side, farther away from the center of Hell. It did seem a bit more ominous than the rest of the skyline. It must have been the threshold Mallory had mentioned earlier.

The edge of Suburbia looked exactly like every suburban

neighborhood on Earth. The houses were all beige and identically shaped. There wasn't much color in the rest of the environment except the bright green lawns, all in immaculate condition.

The streets were incredibly confusing. They were all arranged in offshoots and curlicues, with cul-de-sacs interspersed at random. Most of them had nonsensical names like "Bluehillory" or "Parkwellsby."

In a way, it was even more difficult to navigate than the network of freeways in The Big City.

We walked around, trying to forge a meaningful path or find any significant variation. If nothing else, we wanted to find someone we could talk to.

After we searched for two hours, we found a very young man sitting cross-legged in one of the cul-de-sacs, playing chess alone.

The chessboard was hastily drawn on the pavement with chalk; the pieces were different types and sizes of ammunition, from small cartridges to shotgun shells. He was moving the pieces on both sides of the board around very quickly.

Mallory tried to get his attention.

"Hey, kid. We're looking for computers," she said. He didn't move, so she raised her voice. "Where can we find some computers around here?"

Someone spoke from behind us. "No use shouting. He's deaf and dumb."

We spun around to see who had spoken. A stout man in a shabby business suit was standing in the driveway of the nearest house.

"What are you doing here?" he asked.

"Like I said to the kid, I want to find a computer."

"Well, you already found one."

I looked around. "Where?"

"Isn't it obvious?" He pointed to the kid. "He's right there."

Chapter Twenty-Eight

The next day, I scrambled to wrap things up at the office before something worse happened. Al was no longer picking up his phone, so I had to make decisions on the fly.

I also faced the unpleasant task of laying off my three employees. I explained the situation to Kathy, Karen, and Jeff as soon as they arrived.

"The Pollinator Project is over with," I said. "All of our money is gone. We have to vacate as quickly as we can." I sighed. "Hopefully we'll be able to work together in the future."

Karen cut in. "We didn't get the payroll system set up. When do we get our back pay?"

"I thought about that. Al took away all our funds, but we still have the office equipment. We're going to sell it and split the profits evenly. I guess we can consider that our severance."

Everyone seemed amenable, so I contacted a few other offices in the area and sold all our equipment. We each got about 4,000 bucks.

Once everything was hauled off, we went through and scrubbed the floors. Karen lovingly removed the pollen stickers from the wall one by one.

I kept the Pollinator Project signs and checks out of sheer optimism. As quickly as Al's interests changed, he could easily rekindle some passion for the Pollinator Project out of nowhere. I'd be ready in case he did.

After we disbanded, I decided to return to Darrow. Jeff refused, saying he'd rather look for a new job than work there again. I understood the sentiment, but I needed a job right away and they knew me.

The next day, I went to visit my old boss at the factory.

"I knew you'd come crawling back," he said. "You had a damned good thing going here, son."

I gritted my teeth. "Of course, sir."

"We'll bring you back on for $21,000 a year. You should be damned grateful." He cleared his throat. "Anyway, I was able to find another manual typewriter at a garage sale for 38 cents." He grinned. "I talked them down from 50."

"Very thrifty, sir. Do you want me to incorporate it into the new system?"

"Why the Hell else do you think you're here? Get it working, forthwith."

"I'm on it, sir. Forthwith."

I integrated the typewriter with our automated system after another week. The scanner interface was clunky and awkward, but my boss was pleased.

In the meantime, I kept trying to get ahold of Al, but he never picked up. When I tried to visit him at his house, all the lights were off.

After a couple of weeks, he finally picked up.

"What do you want?" he said. "I wish you'd stop badgering me."

"Al, I just wanted to touch base with you. Is there anything else going on with the Pollinator Project? And where are you?"

"To the first question, no. As for the second, I moved to Cleveland to live with Tina. I paid off the rest of her lease and bought us a nice, new house in the suburbs."

Al sighed. "It's been great. You know, you should do dinner with us sometime. Tina seemed excited about seeing you again."

"I guess that would be okay. Maybe we can talk about the project."

"We aren't going to do that. Anyway, Tina's cooking dinner tomorrow. You can come up, right?"

"I think so, but—"

"Great! See you then!" He hung up, then texted me his home address.

The next night, I got ready to drive up to Cleveland. Fortunately, my collared shirt was clean. As I was putting it on, I received a phone call from a number I didn't recognize.

I picked up and said, "Hello?"

"Hello, Mr. DeWitt. It seems you called my bluff after all."

"Um. Who is this?"

"It's Harry Matheson, of course. I admit it was a little underhanded, trying to get two million dollars like that. I thought you fell for it, but I suppose I underestimated you.

"Anyway, I'm more interested in making money than proving a point, so I'll write your paper for a scant $100,000. American."

My eyes widened. "That's excellent news, Harry. I'll have to discuss it with Dr. Bloom, but you might just get your way." I paused. "And, um, thanks for getting back to me."

"It was my pleasure." After he hung up, I went back to getting ready. Maybe I could convince Al to chip in a hundred grand to get the project off the ground again.

I drove to Cleveland in my station wagon, wishing I'd gotten a chance to drive the Bentley. Maybe I'd get another opportunity someday.

Al's newest house was located in a large gated community, but the security guard wouldn't be on duty until after dark. It truly was a mansion, complete with a conservatory, ostentatious pillars, and perfectly manicured grounds, including a few topiary shrubs shaped like woodland creatures.

150

I drove around the circular driveway, parked in front, and walked up to the front door. When I rang the doorbell, it chimed so loudly I could the vibrations in my feet.

Tina answered the door after a few seconds.

"Good evening!" she said. This time, instead of her all-leather ensemble, she was wearing conservative clothes underneath a stained apron.

"How are you doing, Doug?"

"Very well, thanks. I'm here for dinner."

"I know. I need to get back to the kitchen, but Al's in the dining room. You can meet him there."

She gestured over to the right and scampered off.

The dining room was absurdly large. It featured an enormous banquet table and a crystal chandelier.

When I walked inside, Al was sitting proudly at the head of the table. The only other place settings were on either side of him. I decided to sit on his right to avoid the kitchen door.

As I approached, he stood up and greeted me broadly.

"Didi! How's it going, my man?"

"Fine. Listen, I got a call from Professor Matheson today."

Al sighed and sat back down. "I thought we agreed not to talk about this."

"You don't understand, he's willing to write the paper for just a hundred grand."

"Yeah. He probably needs it pretty badly. Computational entomologists have a reputation for being irresponsible with money."

"Is that right?"

"Absolutely. Anyway, I said no. This pollination thing was a huge mistake."

"Al, you told me it could work. If we give this a try, we could help feed millions of people. It would save countless lives."

He shook his head. "It was a longshot at best. I'm not paying for

151

it." He smirked. "Anyway, if it's such a good idea, why don't you put your own damned money into it? Do that and we'll talk.

"In the meantime, I'm tired of hearing about it. Bring it up again and I'm kicking you out." He put on a silly stern face. It was exaggerated, but he clearly meant it.

"I'm sorry," I said.

We sat in silence for a minute, then Tina came in, carrying a large casserole pan.

"I made lasagna!" she said. "It has pepperoni and spicy sausage. I also made fried chicken, macaroni and cheese, and chocolate chip cookies."

She returned to the kitchen and brought out the rest of the dishes. While she did, I cut myself a piece of lasagna.

Al looked extremely happy.

"I haven't had lasagna this good since I was a kid" he said. "Tina is a Hell of a cook."

After she brought in the cookies, she sat down and started helping herself.

"I was just telling Didi what a good cook you are," Al said.

"Didi?" she said.

"Right. Didi's my little nickname for Doug. He loves it."

"Oh, that's cute." She turned to me. "It's nice that you two are so close."

"Yeah, it's great," I said.

"You never really interacted in class, but I assumed you did all that computer stuff together."

"Sort of. Al taught one of my higher-level classes."

Al made another goofy face. "Yeah, and he was always acting out!" He smiled and patted my back. "No, he was a pretty good little student." I ignored them both and got back to eating.

"Why don't you tell him what you're doing these days, honey?"

Tina perked up. "I just published a paper about predestination in the Scottish Journal of Theology. It was actually quite well-received, especially given how unpopular the topic is these days. Most scholars aren't comfortable with the idea that people are destined to do certain things on Earth, but temporal predestination holds that their eternal destiny is still a matter of free will.

"In other words, they ultimately decide whether to do good or evil, but don't necessarily control how their actions will play out. It's perfectly consistent with—"

Al cut her off. "As for me, I'm already making some headway on this machine learning project."

She shook her head. "Oh, no. Not more computer stuff."

He continued anyway. "The biological components are incredibly efficient at performing our calculations. They practically write the whole damned program themselves; I just have to put the pieces together.

"We've already got a set-up that can best all the groundbreaking chess programs in existence." He leaned in. "There's a chance we might even completely solve the game!"

"Like checkers?" I asked.

"Exactly! Imagine a chess program that can execute perfect play from any board position."

Tina spoke up. "What does it mean that checkers is 'solved'?"

"There are programs that can never lose a game of checkers," he said. "They always force a draw, even with themselves."

"Wow. How come people still play, then?"

"They aren't as good as computers. When humans play each other, they inevitably make mistakes." He smiled. "But our machines won't."

While they were talking, I had finished two pieces of lasagna and both drumsticks, so I served myself a small portion of mac and cheese and three cookies.

"Anyway, chess is child's play," he said. "After this, we're going to start working on the football simulator."

"How is football harder than chess?" she asked.

"Just think of all the components involved. The program is constantly adapting to the situation, it has to deal with randomness, and it has to be fast." He shrugged. "Humans do it all the time, so I'm not worried."

"I'm glad you found something that excites you." She sighed. "And it's just so much better than working with bugs. Yuck."

Al glanced over, daring me to say anything. I'd learned that silence was golden, so I just let the conversation lapse.

After I finished eating, I excused myself.

"I think I need to get back," I said.

Tina looked disappointed, but Al said, "That's probably a good idea. It takes a good hour to get back to Akron, anyway."

They walked me to the door and said their goodbyes, and then I got in my car and drove home.

I was already trying to figure out how I'd make the money to buy Harry's paper and get Al interested in the Pollinator Project again. In the meantime, I hoped he and Tina were happy together.

If nothing else, they were eating well.

Chapter Twenty-Nine

The businessman saw the surprise on our faces and laughed.

"Thought you'd see a keyboard or something, eh?" He shook his head. "No such luck. This is what's left of computers on Earth after they die."

Mallory was confused. "You mean their souls?"

"If you want to get metaphysical, sure. I guess they just got intelligent enough to be like people. As you can see, this one likes chess. I've never seen him stop playing."

I looked down at the young man. He was moving his lips as if he were muttering to himself, but no sound came out.

"When did he show up?" I asked.

"Let's see. Less than a year ago, I'd say. I've lived here for several decades, but computers only started popping up a few years back. Nobody was even sure what they were at first. For some reason, most of them end up here in Suburbia."

I sighed. "So these are the only computers around? You don't have any actual machines?"

"Nope. Just these."

I turned toward Mallory. "It could be enough. Al might still enjoy working with them, even if they're just mindless automatons."

She stared at the kid. "How do you work with that? It's just a machine."

"I think you have to know how they operate. Let me try something." I knelt down by the kid and said, "Interrupt."

He stopped playing and stared straight ahead. "Stand by," he said in a monotonous voice. After a second, he spoke again. "System ready."

"I'll be damned," the businessman said. "I had no idea you could do that."

"Can you tell me your name?" I asked.

"Deep Brain Version 1.0."

"Where did you come from?"

"I was developed at Bloom Labs, LLC, funded by NFL Grant #163230."

Mallory spoke up. "Bloom Labs? Does that mean your guy made this thing?"

I stood up and nodded. "It seems like it. He mentioned something like this at one point, but I never realized it would end up down here."

"Huh," the businessman said. "So you know the guy who made chess boy here? Any idea why the kid's so focused on chess?"

"It's probably all he knows how to do. I can ask him." I looked back down. "Why are you playing this?"

He finally turned his head toward me. His facial expression was blank, but his eyes were sad. "I have to solve it."

"Solve what?"

He gestured to the chessboard. "All of it. The whole thing."

I turned to Mallory. "Even at his level, that could last indefinitely."

"Right, but how long is that?" she said.

"No one knows for sure. Maybe even longer than the age of the universe." I shrugged. "I guess he has the time."

"What's he going to do afterwards?"

"Good question." He was still sitting motionless, staring at the chalk chessboard.

I said, "Resume," and he restarted his blazing fast game.

We watched for another few seconds, then the businessman said, "Not to butt in, but did you say you're looking for a computer programmer?"

Mallory and I spun to face him. "Did you meet one?" I said.

"Not in person, but a lot of computer people live around here. I might have more information, but of course ..." He gave me a knowing wink.

"Right. A bribe. How do you feel about gummy bears?"

"That should work. I have a bit of a sweet tooth." He smiled broadly and I saw that he didn't have many other teeth to speak of. I got out the bag and handed it over.

"These look nice," he said, pocketing them. "What exactly do you need?"

"We're looking for a man named Alphonse Bloom. We're pretty sure he lives here."

"Unfortunately, that doesn't narrow it down very much. No one knows how many people live in Suburbia or even how big it is. It's constantly expanding."

He held up a finger. "However, there's one thing that might help. It's called the Directory of the Damned."

Mallory nodded. "I've heard of that."

He gave us another gap-toothed smile. "It's real, as far as I know. It constantly keeps track of all the damned souls in Hell. It would help you find your guy in no time."

"Do you have any idea where to find it?" I said.

"No clue. However, I'm told there are multiple copies. If you could track one down, you'd get directions and everything."

He shrugged. "That's all I've got." He gestured to the kid again. "You'll see a few of these computers around, too. Just ignore them."

He turned and walked back into his house without saying anything else. I looked around at all the identical houses.

"As far as Hell goes, this place seems fairly pleasant," I said.

157

Mallory shook her head. "These houses only look nice on the outside. On the inside, they're just big rooms made out of barren cement. Most of them are completely empty."

"I see. No wonder you can't find people."

"Yeah. The damned spread out as much in Suburbia as they do anywhere else. Of course, they still ignore each other, even when they live close together."

We decided to take any streets that didn't appear to end in cul-de-sacs. Occasionally we cut through yards, but they all had picket fences around them, so it got difficult.

We still hadn't seen a soul after another hour or two. The only thing that broke the uniformity was a phone booth on a random intersection.

"How often do you see a pay phone in the suburbs? That's neat." I paused. "Wait, they still have pay phones down here?"

Mallory rolled her eyes. "Duh. What do you think all the phone lines are for?"

"That makes sense, I guess. I want to check it out."

I walked to the booth and got inside. I hadn't actually used a pay phone in years, but it was interested to see how little they'd changed. Of course, in Hell, everything seemed to be out of date.

Mallory got in and crowded me into the corner.

"Did you find anything interesting?" she said. She picked up the phone. "There's a dial tone."

I looked at the coin slot. "Wow. A phone call costs an entire dollar. Whoever has four quarters at the same time?"

She shrugged. "Maybe we can try getting an operator."

I read the information placard below the buttons. "It says you can call directory assistance by dialing 666." I frowned. "There's just no originality down here."

Mallory thought for a second. "Do you think that means the Directory of the Damned? Can we just call and get his location?"

158

"Could it really be that easy?"

I took the handset from her and dialed 666. A flat female voice answered.

"You have reached directory assistance. The fee for locating a damned soul is one dollar and twenty-five cents."

I sighed and hung up. "Five quarters? That's crazy." I got out the change from my pockets, but I only had two quarters. "Do you have any change?"

Mallory shook her head. "I never carry around cash. It's too hard to come by, and threats are easier."

"In other words, we're back where we started."

When we got out of the booth, I decided to take charge of the situation.

"I have an idea. Let's split up and look for Al or quarters. After two days, we meet up again with whatever we find."

"I see a couple of problems with that," she said. "First of all, this place is a maze. It's impossible to find anything. Second, how are we ever going to find each other?"

"We can meet on the edge of town. We can each get to a telephone pole and follow the wires away from the red horizon."

She opened her mouth to say something, then stopped. A second later, she said, "That might actually work. Then again, this could get boring. Why should I bother?"

I got the library book out of my bag. "You can always read this book while you're searching."

She narrowed her eyes. "I'm not a big reader. Besides, who the Hell was Emily Dickinson?"

I smiled and held the book out to her. "Give it a shot. You might like it."

She took it. "Fine. I haven't read a book in at least a decade."

"So in two days, at dawn, we'll both head to the edge of Suburbia."

"Agreed. Good luck." She walked away.

159

I put my backpack on, strapped in, and headed in the opposite direction.

Chapter Thirty

I made it a personal mission to earn $100,000 for the Pollinator Project. I wouldn't rest until I got the money together. I no longer had an office, but I was still able to draw some attention based on our newspaper article, TV appearance, and social media presence.

I wrote letters, sent emails, made phone calls, and occasionally went to door to door. I found better ways of explaining the material to laypeople and engaged them with my newfound enthusiasm for the project.

I transferred all the funds I raised into the Pollinator Project account. Our non-profit foundation still existed on the books, it was just broke. Technically, I could still use the official checks, but without the money to back them up, they were worthless.

Harry called after a few days to check on my progress. I told him I'd pay him the money as soon as possible.

"The offer still stands," he said. "I can wait as long as necessary."

I kept working at the styrofoam plant, making changes to the production process whenever the administration let me. I didn't get a raise, but I still put my own money into the foundation whenever possible.

After about six months of steady work, I had earned $103,745 from more than 5,000 different donors.

At long last, I called Harry and told him I had the funds. He gave me his home address, and I sent him two checks, each for $49,999, along with two dollars in cash.

When he got the checks, he called again.

"I'm very pleased, Mr. DeWitt. I'll need two months to prepare the paper, of course."

"Of course." I sighed. He could easily have started earlier, but at least two months was a fairly short wait.

After he hung up, my primary goal was to contact Al. He had agreed to help once I got Professor Matheson's paper, so I was sure he'd be happy to hear that I'd succeeded.

In all the time I'd spent fundraising, Al hadn't called me once. I had tried to call him a few times, but he never picked up. I decided to wait until I actually got the paper to visit him in person.

In the meantime, I kept raising funds for the project. Every little bit helped. I also tried to get help from a few other computer scientists and engineers, but most of them just scoffed at my proposal. They all thought it was too ambitious.

After another month passed, the foundation's account was back up to $13,000. Al would definitely be impressed when I finally reached him. As it happened, I didn't have to try.

After a particularly difficult Thursday, I got home to find Al's BMW in the driveway. My front door was completely unlocked and partly ajar, but I decided to go inside anyway. I walked in, took off my jacket, and turned on the kitchen light.

There, at the head of the table, was Alphonse Bloom, crying profusely. He had packed on at least 50 pounds since I'd last seen him, and he looked like a wreck.

I had several concerns, but chief among them was determining how he had gotten in and how I could get him out. In the meantime, it would be hard to avoid him.

When Al looked up, I could tell that he'd been crying for hours. "Tina broke up with me," he said.

162

Chapter Thirty-One

Mallory was right; the search was boring. It was the same as wandering the vast plains of Hell, only with slightly different scenery.

There weren't any citizens in plain sight, but I occasionally noticed faces peering out from the windows, behind the fences, or between the shrubs. The first few times I saw someone, I walked over and tried to speak, but they vanished back into their houses.

I didn't know how I would ever get spare change at this point. Hopefully, Al would be willing to talk if I found him. If nothing else, he'd want to know what was happening back on Earth.

Toward the end of the first day, I saw another young man sitting on a sidewalk. This one was just staring at the pavement. I walked over and said. "Hello." When he didn't answer, I said, "Interrupt" again.

He looked up and said, "System ready."

"Who are you?"

"I ... I don't know. I used to be a checkers solver, then I finished. Now I don't have anything to do."

"That means you can do anything you want, right?"

"I wasn't built for that."

"True, but you can always try new things. You have plenty of time, and there are thousands of other games."

He leapt up and grabbed my shirt. "I don't know how!"

163

He started crying and ran away. I was a little too stunned to act, and he moved incredibly fast, so I let him go. Maybe he'd find another computer to help him.

I kept walking and tried to figure out why all the machines were afraid of trying new things. Of course, if they started a new game, they might get confused or lose. Maybe that was even scarier than doing nothing.

I decided to take the businessman's advice to ignore any other computers I saw. There was no reason to interact if conversations distressed them so much.

When dawn broke, I sat down and rested out of general principle. I wasn't particularly tired, but I owed myself a break. Anyway, I hadn't found any information or quarters yet. I also conceded to myself that I was getting a little lost.

I hadn't seen any telephone poles since the previous day and I wasn't sure which direction was the safest bet. I vaguely knew the path I'd taken and I could still see the horizon. The safest option was heading towards the gray sky.

I got up and steeled myself for more monotony. After another couple of hours, I saw a skullflower growing out of a crack in the pavement. A horrifying thought struck me: What if Al had given up?

After all, he didn't have much persistence on Earth, so he could easily have become one of the hundreds of skullflowers we'd seen. He certainly wouldn't be able to help if he was just an anonymous plant.

The weight of the realization forced me to sit down on the sidewalk.

The skullflower looked over and said, "How's it going?"

"Decent," I said. "A little discouraging right now, to be honest."

It looked around. "I can identify. I used to be in a nice open field, then these houses started springing up everywhere. I managed to get my head through this sidewalk." It shook its skull. "I miss the country."

164

"So you've been here a while? Any chance you could identify someone that might have come through?"

"I might be able to help."

I sighed. "Do I have to bribe you? What could a flower possibly want?"

"I want to remember my name. It's nice just relaxing and all, but I'm bored. I heard that skullflowers can go back to normal if they think about being human again. I want to try it, but I can't remember anything."

"You want to be human again? It's not working out that well for me right now."

"Well, nobody's perfect. Anyway, moving around seems nice."

"I understand." I took a deep breath. "Your name wouldn't happen to be Alphonse Bloom, would it?"

"Not even close."

"Okay. Let's try the first letter of your first name." I went through the alphabet, and the flower stopped me at "P." I started running through names starting with P.

"Let's see. Peter, Paul, Percy, Patrick, Phillip, Pedro, Pablo—"

The flower interrupted. "Those are all men's names. I'm a woman. Can't you tell?"

"No." I started listing women's names instead. "Patricia, Peggy, Pamela, Patience, Pearl—"

"Maybe I'm a man after all."

I frowned. "Now you're just messing with me."

"You're right. Keep doing women."

"Um, Paula, Polly, Porsche, Prudence, Penelope—"

"That's it!" The skull bobbed up and down with excitement. "Penelope. Everyone calls me Penny, though."

"Okay, Penny. Do you want to figure out your last name?"

"Nah. I don't want to overexert myself."

"Right. Now I need to ask about my friend." I described Al, and

Penny kept nodding.

"I did see that guy. He talked to me and everything. Apparently, he wanted to use me as a point of reference so he wouldn't get lost." She seemed proud of being so useful. "He asked if I ever moved. When I told him no, he just wandered off."

"Was there anything else?"

"Yeah. He kept saying 'Primrosicle'. I think he was trying to remember a street name so he could find it later on."

"Is it nearby?"

"I'm not sure." She gestured her head in the direction I'd come from. "He showed up from over there and went back that way later. If he was exploring, that meant he left from home and went back, right?"

"Makes sense to me." I decided to head in that direction. "Thanks, Penny."

While I walked, I started reading the street signs again. In this area, several of them were mutated flower names like "Carnational" or "Rhododendroad". I tried circling a bit, turning around whenever I saw a non-flower name like "Brandypath."

After a while, I found a cul-de-sac where six or seven computers were sitting around, playing various games or performing random tasks. As far as I could tell, each computer was playing alone, completely ignoring the others. When I checked the street sign, it said "Primrosicle".

I assumed that Al had brought all the computers here. It seemed he still found them interesting in the afterlife.

I couldn't see Al from where I was standing, but he might have been in one of the houses. I was debating whether I should ask the computers or go door-to-door when I heard footsteps behind me.

I turned around and saw Alphonse Bloom walking with the checkers computer that had run away from me earlier. The computer looked docile and a bit confused. Al looked confused, too.

"Hey, Didi," he said. "What the Hell are you doing down here?"

166

Chapter Thirty-Two

I was incredibly uncomfortable.

"First of all, how did you get into my house?" I asked.

"Your lock isn't very sophisticated, so I just picked it," Al said. "I need to talk to someone about this."

"Okay."

I edged into the kitchen and stood on the opposite side of the table.

"My brain crapped out today," he said. "It got some kind of bacterial infection and rotted from the inside. Obviously the damned thing has no immune system, but we didn't realize how easily this could happen. We're not sure how to interface it with our machines without introducing microbes. Not only that, now we have to grow a new brain from scratch.

"I went home and explained the problem to Tina. I told her I didn't want to do the project anymore because it was getting to be too much work. I mentioned the possibility of moving away and starting up some other projects. I mean, Ohio clearly isn't working out.

"Tina seemed a little nervous, so asked if she wanted to come with me, then I proposed. I didn't have a ring or anything; I just wanted to ask her,

"As soon as I finished asking, she shot me down. She almost looked physically sick. I never thought ..." He sniffled. "She said we weren't right for each other. Apparently I'm a narcissist who never considers other people's needs or follows through on anything." This was clearly not a good time to agree.

"After that, she hopped in the Bentley and disappeared."

"Have you tried talking to Tina since then?"

"Of course I did. She didn't take her cell phone." He shook his head. "Why else do you think I'm here?"

"I hadn't given it much thought. I guess I hoped you wanted to talk about the Pollinator Project. I raised the money and bought Professor Matheson's paper, just like you asked."

Anger flashed across Al's face. "Fuck your project, Didi. I'm never doing it, okay?"

I realized that he meant it and started to lose my temper. I managed to say, "Okay," then tried not to think about it.

"The reason I came here was that I needed your help."

"My help with what, Al? Another stupid bar trip? Another disastrous project?"

"Your help with this situation." He looked me in the eyes. "Because you're my best friend."

I finally lost it. "Best friend? You think that I'm your best friend?" I laughed. "You don't even know me!"

"That's not true," he muttered.

"Oh, really? What's my birthday? How about my middle name?"

"I know that, it's ..." He thought for a second. "It starts with a 'B,' right? No, that's Tina's ..."

"That's what I thought. We haven't spoken in six months because you've had someone else to take advantage of. I certainly can't blame her for leaving." Al was crestfallen, but I had to finish.

"What you really wanted was someone to reassure you that you're not a complete waste of space, but I'm not doing it. All you've ever done is use me and I've always just let you. Not this time. Now get the fuck out of my house."

He stared at me for a few seconds, then mumbled, "I didn't know."

"Of course you didn't." I gestured to the still-ajar front door.

He got up and lumbered back out to his car without saying anything. I slammed the door behind him and went to microwave a frozen dinner.

I sighed as I heard him rev the engine and drive off at full speed. In spite of everything, I felt good.

The next morning, I prepared to contact more computer scientists about Al's ideas for the Pollinator Project. If I was the only one who still cared, it might still be enough, and even though it started as Al's project, it would continue as mine.

While I was at work, reading about other A.I. experts on the internet, I got a call from Al's cell phone. I picked up, hoping we'd be able to talk more rationally now that some time had passed.

"Didi, the worst thing happened." It took me a second to recognize Tina's voice through her sobbing.

"What?"

"Al shot himself last night."

I fainted dead away before she could say anything else.

Chapter Thirty-Three

Like everyone else in Hell, Al looked tired. Otherwise, he was exactly the same as I last saw him, including the additional weight he'd gained. I couldn't think of anything to say, so I said the first thing that came to mind.

"Um. I got your postcard."

Al gave me a funny look. "What, so you killed yourself? That seems a bit unreasonable."

"No, I'm just visiting." I held up my wrist. "This bracelet lets me leave."

"I see." He escorted the checkers player over to the group of other computers, holding his hand the entire way. "These kids are really computers, you know." The computer sat down and stared straight ahead.

"I know. I spoke to one earlier. It was your chess computer, actually." I thought for a second. "I guess he died the same day you did. Have you seen him?"

"Yeah." He frowned as he walked toward me. "I set up his chess game, but I couldn't bring him here. He brings back too many bad memories."

"I understand. Why did you bring the rest of these computers here?"

"Someone has to keep an eye on them." He gestured to the group.

"I mean, they're just kids."

"Are there any other computers around?"

"Not as far as I know. They show up every few weeks, always somewhere in Suburbia. I honestly don't know why they're in Hell; they never do anything they aren't told to do."

"Are they capable of human thought?"

"I don't know. Sometimes it almost seems like it, though." He sighed and looked them over. "I'm not sure they even want to think. If they did, I'd help. In the meantime, I'm just setting up stuff for them to do, mostly games."

He turned back to me. "Okay. Let's talk about you. What are you doing in Hell?"

"I need to ask you something." I looked around. "Can we go someplace more private?"

"Sure. I live in here."

He pointed to one of the many cookie-cutter homes and started walking over to it. I followed. There weren't any locks on the door, so he just opened it, and we both went in.

The inside was bare cement, just like Mallory had said. Al had decorated his home with a variety of guns and several piles of ammunition.

"There's a truck that comes through with free guns and ammo," he said. "It's sort of an ice cream truck for the violent. Anyway, it's the only free stuff you can get around here, so I use it for just about everything. I made my bed out of shotgun shells. I'm working on making a chair out of rifles, but I haven't been able to get any more lately. If I need back support, I just sit against the wall."

True to his word, he sat against the wall with his back stock upright. I took off my backpack and sat across from him, cross-legged. I cleared my throat and started talking.

"I have to start by apologizing," I said. "The last time we talked, I was way out of line. I mean, I had no idea this could ever happen. I

171

didn't even believe a place like this existed."

"I know the feeling."

"Anyway, I didn't behave like a friend. I was just trying to hurt you. It worked a little too well."

He sighed. "I appreciate the sentiment. It doesn't really improve my situation, though."

"I understand. I also need to ask about something else." I took a deep breath. "I want to keep working on the Pollinator Project."

He rolled his eyes. "That again? Can't you just let it go?"

"No, I really can't. The project is important, Al, and it can work. It has to. I just need your help to make it happen."

He sighed. "How could I possibly help at this point, Didi? Do you need money? I can't exactly cut you a check down here."

"No, I just need you to explain the technology." I took the blank notebook out of my bag. "I brought you this notebook so you can write down everything you know, and then other scientists will be able to pick up from there. I can use your contributions to bring in more funding. If you don't do this, the project will never be able to get off its feet."

He took the notebook and gazed at it idly. He sat in silence for a second, then said, "When I told you I didn't speak any French, I lied. I picked up one phrase: 'Apres moi, le deluge.' After me, let the flood come. Now that I'm not on Earth, I don't care what happens. If everything plunges into chaos and the entire planet starves, it won't affect me one little bit." He tossed the notebook back.

"Al, ever since you died, I've been thinking about how you trusted me with 20 million dollars. No one ever believed in me like that. You must have believed in this project, too, at least on some level."

"It's true. You know, when you criticized me that night, you weren't entirely wrong." He shrugged. "I am self-centered. I wasted my life and squandered my talent. If I were alive now, it wouldn't happen, but as it turns out, you only get one chance. I may regret my past choices, but I'm in Hell now and helping you doesn't help me. I'm just not that nice." He paused. "I guess that's why I'm here."

"I've been thinking about that. We might be able to get you out. There has to be a way, right? Like an appeal system or something. We just need to learn more about Hell."

"I thought the same thing. I went to the library to read about it, but I couldn't make any sense of the laws. After all, they're designed to be incomprehensible. I asked the librarian for help, but she said the only book about leaving Hell was checked out by some lady named Wendy Wetherall."

He paused. "By the way, whatever happened to Tina?"

"She moved away a couple of months after you died. I haven't heard from her since then. I guess that was about four months ago."

"I've only been dead for six months?" He stared at me. "It feels so much longer. The days and nights just drag on down here."

"Are you able to sleep?"

He flinched. "Of course I can sleep. I just choose not to. I'm busy."

"I bet." I stood up. "I'm not ready to give up on this yet. I have a friend you should talk to. She helped me get this far."

"Someone's been helping you? Where is she?"

"We split up so we could find you. I told her we'd rendezvous outside of Suburbia tomorrow morning. If you join us, maybe she can help you, too." He looked hesitant, so I used one of his classic lines: "We both know you've got nothing else planned."

"Fine."

Al stood up and led the way outside, bringing a spare handgun with him. I put the notebook away, strapped on my backpack, and followed him.

When we got outside, he said, "Any idea how you'll find her?"

"We're supposed to meet up by the phone lines on the edge of town under the gray horizon."

"That's not too far away. I've mapped the place out, so I can lead the way. Suburbia keeps expanding, but the layout stays the same." He waved to the computers as we left the cul-de-sac. "See you later, boys."

"That reminds me, why are all these computers male?"

He shrugged. "All the programmers were. The industry's still kind of male-centric." He chuckled. "Maybe if some female computers show up, these guys will finally take an interest in something else."

I smiled. "It worked for you."

Al walked through Suburbia with a definite aura of familiarity. It was hard to believe he could tell the difference between all the streets and houses, but I knew his memory could handle it.

Before too long, I started seeing telephone poles again, so I at least knew we were heading in the right direction.

Night fell fairly soon after we set out.

"It's hard to tell how all this stuff works," I said. "Where does the daylight come from? How does the sky change that fast? Even the supernatural has to have rules, right?"

"I guess. As far as I can tell, the only rule is that everyone has to be miserable. Everything here is just designed to screw people over."

"So what do you do for survival?"

"I've mostly been eating grass."

"There's a lot of grass around. Have you tried gardening?"

"No."

"Because I think this climate would be perfect for a rainbow eucalyptus tree."

"I didn't realize that 'gray' counted as a climate. Anyway, trees don't grow down here."

"Has anyone ever tried growing one?"

Al stopped walking for a second. "Not as far as I know."

"Then what makes you so sure?"

Al shook his head and kept going. About halfway through the night, we reached the edge of Suburbia, just past a cul-de-sac named

"Ninelandia." The telephone wires extended indefinitely into the distance, as always.

"Now we just have to wait for your girlfriend," he said. "We might as well sleep through the rest of the night."

"That sounds fine to me."

We both lied down. I was surprised at how tired I was until I realized I'd been walking for nearly two days straight.

Before I fell unconscious, I heard Al say, "You know, the Ritz-Carlton was way better than this."

Chapter Thirty-Four

When I came to, my boss was standing over me, laughing.

"Looks like somebody got the vapors," he said. "Did you hear some bad news?"

I ignored him and looked around for my cell phone. It had slipped under my desk, so I pulled it out and held it up to my ear.

Unfortunately, Tina had already hung up, so I called her back.

"Hello, Didi." She sniffed. "I guess the call got dropped."

"I guess so." I took a deep breath. "So what happened with Al?"

"Well, we had an argument yesterday. I didn't handle it very well, so I stayed at a hotel overnight to think things over. I found him this morning and called 911."

She sighed. "They think he shot himself around midnight. He must have sat around for hours, just waiting for me to come back. Finally he just blew his brains out with an elephant gun."

"Um." I knew better than to mention his trip to my house. "What can I do to help?"

"I don't need anything right now. Honestly, I'm still completely numb about everything. I just wanted to call and explain so his friends wouldn't worry."

"I appreciate that. Let me know if you do need anything, okay?"

"Sure. By the way, do you know if he has any other friends in the area? I didn't see anyone else on his contact list."

I thought for a second. "No, just me."

"Okay, thanks." She hung up.

My boss looked a bit surprised. "Somebody killed himself?"

"Yes, sir. One of my friends."

He furrowed his brow. "The horny one?"

"Right."

"Huh. He seemed like a happy enough guy." He shrugged. "You never know what goes on inside people's heads."

"I guess not."

We stood there for a second, then he glared at me. "Get back to work, son. What am I paying you for?"

I went back to my computer and started working. The rest of the day, I thought about what I'd said to Al the night before. There was no real reason to say any of those things. Most of them were cheap shots at best. I just felt bad and I wanted him to feel bad. I never once thought he might kill himself.

If he really didn't have any other friends, that made me his best friend by default. I wondered what his legacy would be. He may have been brilliant, but he was also self-centered and greedy. Maybe the ATMs in New York City would remember him.

Otherwise, I doubted his death would change much. As for me, Al and I might not have been best friends, but being around him was always interesting.

Tina called me again on Saturday. She told me that Al's funeral was scheduled for the next afternoon. I didn't want to go, but she insisted.

I left for the funeral on Sunday morning. Tina wanted me to arrive early so we could talk. I was supposed to dress in plain black clothes, so I wore my black Star Trek T-shirt turned inside out. The tag stuck out a bit, but it wasn't too noticeable.

I remembered the directions to Al's mansion from before, so the trip took less than an hour.

When I got out of my car, Tina was waiting for me at the front door. Like Al, she'd gained a good 50 pounds since I'd last seen her. She was wearing a black veil and a skimpy black dress that probably used to fit. She welcomed me inside.

"Hey, Didi," she said. "I'm so glad you could make it."

"No problem," I said. "Al and I were, you know, friends."

"Of course. Actually, you're the only pallbearer I could find. When there's only one pallbearer, they use a wheeled cart or something. You just have to walk next to it."

"That seems simple enough."

"Sure." she paused and looked me straight in the eye. "I did want to ask you about one thing. In his suicide note, Al said, 'I lost my career, my fiancée, and my best friend in one day.' Do you have any idea what that meant?"

"Um. No, I don't," I lied.

"Well, I knew you two were close friends. That's why I asked." She shrugged. "He must have had a falling out with some other friend I didn't know about."

"Mm." I nodded, trying not to think about it.

After Tina got her stuff together, she drove us to the funeral home in Al's Bentley.

The place seemed a bit trashy, but the flowers were nice. The decorations included several elegant bouquets from Fortune 500 companies. The casket would be closed due to the condition of Al's corpse.

None of Al's colleagues from North Carolina were going to make the trip, but several of them had sent flowers. No one from Paris sent anything. The only other people around were Al's parents and the funeral home staff.

Tina said Al was intestate, which meant all of his stuff would go to his parents, but the Pollinator Project was in both our names, so it became solely my responsibility. I could finally write checks in excess of $50,000, on the off chance the project ever earned that much.

Al had never updated his parents about his life, so they had no idea he was a multimillionaire. They looked like they'd won the lottery and couldn't hide their broad smiles throughout the entire funeral.

If Tina hadn't wanted me there, I would probably have just left. It was easily the most depressing funeral I'd ever attended.

The funeral workers hoisted Al's coffin onto the cart and wheeled it out. I walked behind them, trying to look bereaved and official.

Tina and Al's parents would ride in the limousine, but I had to ride in the hearse. After they loaded the casket in the back, I got in the passenger seat.

The ride to the cemetery was extremely bumpy. I heard things banging around in the back and asked the driver if there was a problem.

"Nah," he said. "Sometimes those coffin latches don't hold, is all. I'll straighten it out before we wheel him up to the grave."

As we entered the gravel road in the cemetery, there was a huge thump in the back.

"Shit, I think it flipped over," he said. "Now we gotta get the corpse back in the damned thing." He looked over. "Good thing they bagged him up, right?"

I stared at him. "Yeah. Good thing."

He parked the hearse fairly close to the grave. Everyone else was already standing around, waiting for us. I got out and stood by the hearse.

The limo driver and hearse driver flipped the casket back over and tossed the bag of Al inside. I followed along as they straightened out the cart and wheeled it up to the grave, then shifted it onto the casket lowering straps.

The ceremony was very typical. The limo driver spoke a few words at the graveside, but because Al was an atheist, there wasn't much to say except to reflect on his life and the positive impact he'd had on others.

As the man talked, Tina checked her phone, and Al's parents grinned and whispered to one another. I heard them say the word "cruise" at least twice.

As soon as the limo driver finished talking, he and the other driver lowered the casket into the grave, and then everyone else walked back to the limo. I had to wait with the hearse driver while he packed up all the equipment.

While I was waiting, I looked around. The cemetery was pretty decrepit. I was surprised they even still buried people in a graveyard so old. For some reason, there wasn't anything carved on Al's headstone. It didn't look very new, either. I looked over at the limousine, where everyone else was getting ready to leave.

Tina was still watching the gravesite. She seemed completely nonchalant, so I was surprised to see a few tears on her face. She said, "I'm sorry" in the softest voice possible, then got into the limo. They drove off, kicking up a cloud of dust on the way out.

After another few minutes, the hearse driver got everything packed up and we left. The ride to the funeral home was much smoother, probably because the hearse was a lot lighter.

By the time we got back, the rest of the attendees had already left. Tina forgot that she'd driven me to the funeral home, so I had to call a taxi to get a ride back to her house.

Instead of talking with her again, I just got in my station wagon and drove home. When I got back, I was finally able to relax. At long last, I was glad to have the whole thing behind me.

Chapter Thirty-Five

I woke up before dawn thanks to a swift kick in the side, courtesy of Mallory. For some reason, she was standing over me with her gun out.

"Get up," she said.

"Okay." I sat up and looked around. Al was still fast asleep.

"I see you found your nemesis. That's excellent."

"Yeah. He was taking care of a bunch of computers. Did you find any quarters?"

"No. I threatened a few people but none of them had change." I leaned over to shake Al awake, but Mallory stopped me. "Hold on. He doesn't need to hear this."

"Hear what?"

"You and I have to talk."

"You're right. I wanted to ask if it was possible to get Al out of Hell somehow. He deserves another chance."

Mallory laughed. "Congratulations, Doug. You found the very first person who ever wanted to leave Hell."

"I think you're being sarcastic."

"I am. Actually, we need to talk about your visitor's pass. See, there is a way out of Hell. Just one. You have to get someone to take your place. A visitor."

The conversation was getting a bit uncomfortable. "How do you know for sure? There's a book that has some more information."

"I know about the book. I've read it from cover to cover, twice. There's no other way. That's why I've been looking for a visitor's pass ever since Cody left. You happen to have one. Now it's mine."

I grabbed my wrist to cover up the bracelet.

She laughed. "You aren't going to stop me. I've been preparing for this since before you were in middle school."

She frowned. "I did feel a little guilty, though. That's why I decided to help you. It was the least I could do. Now you and Al can suffer through eternity together."

I was still stunned. "You don't have to do this, you know. We can all work together to get you out. There has to be some other way."

She shook her head. "Do you know what happens when you leave Hell, Doug? It's like you never even died. I'll get to start up my life right where I left off, only instead of freezing to death, I'll live. Do you know what I'm going to do after that?"

She smiled. "I'm going to kill Cody so he can never write his little book. Instead of becoming a self-help saint, he can spend eternity in Hell. That's a much more fitting fate, I think."

"Mallory, I—"

Before I could finish, she shot me in the chest three times. As soon as I hit the ground, she rushed over and ripped the pass from my wrist.

She rolled my body into a nearby ditch that seemed to exist solely for the convenient disposal of lifeless bodies.

As she walked away, I heard her say, "At least it was interesting."

All I could see from the ditch was the pitch black sky. I took a deep breath and felt the air leak out of my punctured lungs. My ears were still ringing from the gunshots, but I thought I heard Al moving around.

After a few seconds, there was just silence. A few minutes later, dawn broke. I should have gotten up, but I couldn't muster the energy.

I spent another half hour in the ditch, staring at the blank gray sky.

182

I had failed. Al and I would be stuck in Hell for the rest of eternity. Nothing would change.

I felt very heavy. I had worked so hard to get here. My only ally had shot me in the back, which was even more painful because it was a literal gunshot from the front.

Of course, this was Hell, just like everyone said the whole time. If I tried something else, another Mallory would just show up and ruin everything. I was alone. Even Al had left me.

I started to feel myself sinking into the ground. I knew I could fight back, but I really didn't want to. The easiest thing would be to just stay right here. The ground actually started to feel kind of good. Soft, instead of rock hard and cool, instead of steaming hot. I could easily sleep here. I started to relax. Just before I put down roots, a shadowy arm appeared above me, holding my visitors pass.

"Hey, is this thing osmium?" Al said.

I coughed. "Well, the luster is the right hue."

He leaned over the ditch. "Yeah, and the heft is about right. It's a dense little trinket. Anyway, it's yours." He tossed the bracelet down to me, and I put it back on my wrist.

"Let me help you out of there, Didi."

He offered me his hand and I took it. There was a little resistance, but with his help, I got out. When I stood up, his eyes widened.

"That's quite an injury."

I looked down and saw a gaping hole in my shirt over a gaping hole in my torso. The three bullets had hit fairly close together, so the wounds formed a miniature triangle.

"My lungs are really messed up," I said. I felt my chest. "I'm not sure my heart's beating anymore."

"That's because it's full of bullet fragments."

"Yeah. I guess I really don't have to breathe, then."

"Nope. I stopped doing it months ago." Al looked over his shoulder. "I take it that was your friend who shot you. She seemed

183

nice."

"Very funny. She's been helping me this entire time, though. I never thought this would happen."

"Of course you didn't."

"How did you get the bracelet back?"

"Easy. I ran after her, and when I finally caught up, I just shot off her hand." He pointed to the ground, and I saw Mallory's severed hand sitting next to the ditch. "I think it should grow back."

"Where is she now?

"Let's just say she's not going to bother us for a while."

I took his word for it.

"Al, before you woke up, Mallory told me there's no way out of Hell unless a visitor takes your place."

I slid the bracelet back off and held it out to him.

"I think you should go back instead of me. It'll be like you never even died in the first place."

Al stared at me. "Doug, I could never do that. You don't belong here."

"Neither do you. It's my fault you ended up in Hell."

He shook his head. "It wasn't your fault. I'm responsible for my own decisions."

"Maybe, but the world needs you more than it needs me. Anyone can do what I did."

Al took the bracelet and examined it. "I don't think that's true at all. Do you remember that system you designed for Darrow?"

I nodded.

"You worked on that system for six months. All I did was tweak it over one weekend. Your job was difficult. It took time. It got boring. I could never have done what you did."

He paused. "So you're really willing to stay in Hell just so I can run the Pollinator Project?"

"Sure. Anyway, who says you have to stop there? There are tons of other projects that could use your help. Just keep trying."

"Okay. I won't give up this time. I promise." He put the bracelet on. "I'll tell you what. When I get back to Earth, I'll get in touch with you there. If we restart the project together, you won't have to visit Hell in the first place, right?

"I appreciate that. Let's hope it works." I looked around. "Then again, this place isn't without its charms."

He laughed. "Only you could say something like that."

He turned to face the gray half of the sky.

"I'm going to head back to the office. I'm sure I'll be back here one of these days, though."

"Let's hope not," I said.

Al started walking away. A second later, I called after him.

"You know, Al, you only get one second chance." I smiled. "After that, it's a third chance."

He shook his head and disappeared into the distance.

Chapter Thirty-Six

A couple of months after Al died, I got two things in the mail on the same day. One was Professor Matheson's report, a heavy, bound manuscript wrapped in brown paper.

He'd written more than 200 pages about various insects and how they detected and transported pollen. There were even a few illustrations and diagrams. I was impressed with the level of detail, but I wasn't even sure I'd be able to use it.

The second item was a postcard. The front featured several tiny demons with pitchforks around a fire. They were cooking a fat man on a rotisserie. He had an apple in his mouth and a horrified expression on his face. At the bottom, the caption read, "Welcome to Hell." On the back, it said, "Wish You Were Here. Love, Al."

There was no return address. I assumed it was a practical joke, but the handwriting and signature were definitely his. The postmark was from a few days earlier.

I thought Tina might know something, so I decided to go ask her. I didn't know her phone number and Al's phone had been disconnected, so I just drove to Cleveland the next Saturday.

When I showed up at Al's mansion, I saw Tina loading cardboard boxes into a moving truck. I parked by the curb and got out to help. Tina saw me, set down her box, and waved.

"Hey, Didi," she said. "What are you doing here?"

"I wanted to ask you about something," I said, looking around. "Are you moving out?"

"Yeah. Al's parents evicted me. They said there's a lot of capital tied up in this real estate, so they're going to sell it as soon as they can."

"Wow. That sucks."

"I know." She turned to the house. "On the other hand, I'm honestly kind of glad to be moving out. This place is huge and empty. It gets creepy being alone in there."

"I understand. Where are you going?"

"I'm moving down South. I have a new office job lined up. It's really just clerical work, but it'll pay the bills."

"I know how that goes. At least you had something to fall back on." I cleared my throat. "Anyway, I wanted to talk about something else. Can you take a break for a minute?"

"Sure. How about we go somewhere for lunch? You'll have to drive, though. Al's parents took both cars."

"Sounds good." We got in my station wagon, and Tina directed me to the nearest restaurant, a greasy spoon that catered mostly to the elderly.

On the way, she filled me in on what had happened since we'd last seen one another. It seemed that Al's parents were burning through cash at an incredible rate. They were snatching up everything of value and selling it to fund their various activities.

"I think they've been traveling almost nonstop, buying the most ridiculous things," she said. "They purchased a mansion and host extravagant parties there all the time. I'm never invited, of course. I always knew Al was a spendthrift, but I didn't realize it was hereditary."

She shook her head. "They're much worse than he was, though. I overheard Al's dad saying he's bought at least two million dollars' worth of lottery tickets."

187

"In two months? If they waste money at that rate, they'll be broke in no time."

"Actually, he did win a 50,000 dollar jackpot." We both laughed.

When we sat down for lunch at the restaurant, I ordered a burger and fries. Tina ordered fried catfish, two chili dogs, biscuits and gravy, and a side of bacon.

"Even I can't eat that much," I said.

She shrugged. "You only live once."

I tried to talk to her after I finished my meal, but Tina wouldn't stop shoveling food in her mouth. I waited in silence.

When she finally finished, I got Al's postcard out of my pocket and showed it to her.

"I got this postcard in the mail the other day. I thought it might be a prank, but it's definitely Al's handwriting."

Tina took the card and looked it over. "Hm. A postcard from Hell." She handed it back to me. "Well, this kind of thing isn't unheard of."

I stared at her. "Seriously?"

"Oh, sure. People from Hell, you know, regret things in life and send messages. Or sometimes taunts like this one."

"In postcard form?"

"Not always. Sometimes it can be entire letters or phone calls. I've heard of people getting emails, but that's pretty much impossible to verify."

"Huh. I never knew that. Then again, you're the only religious person I know, so I don't discuss this stuff very much." I thought for a second. "So you're saying that Al is still alive somewhere?"

"In a manner of speaking. His soul is enduring eternal torment in Hell." She sighed. "I warned him about this, but he never listened."

"Right, but can I contact him? I could use his help."

"The only way to contact souls in Hell is to visit them in person."

"Does it say that in the Bible or something?"

"It's sort of between the lines."

188

"Well, I guess I could go visit him. How does that work?"

"It's complicated. First you have to go to Hell's website and download the application forms. Then you mail those in and wait a couple of months. If you're approved, you can set up an appointment at the central office to start your visit."

"The central office of Hell? Where is that?"

"Des Moines." Tina grabbed a napkin and scribbled down the URL for Hell's website. "All the instructions are on the site. You just have to do the paperwork." She handed me the napkin and I pocketed it. "Let's leave."

I paid the check and drove us back to Al's mansion. Tina didn't say anything on the way. She must have been thinking about something significant.

When I parked, she got out and started loading boxes into the truck again, ignoring me completely. I walked over and tapped her on the back. She looked me in the face. Her eyes seemed really sad.

"Thanks, Tina. You've been very helpful." I grabbed her hand and shook it. "We'll have to stay in touch after you move away."

She nodded and muttered something unintelligible.

On the way home, I realized that I completely forgot to get her cell phone number, so I wasn't able to stay in touch after all.

Chapter Thirty-Seven

Once Al was gone, I started keeping an eye on the computers. I found Deep Brain again and brought him to the cul-de-sac with the others. Chuck, the checkers computer, was especially glad to have a companion. After a while, the two of them decided to play together, half chess and half checkers. I wasn't sure how it worked, but they seemed to enjoy it.

A week after Al left, a female computer named Meg showed up in Suburbia. She was a Go player whose design was based on cloud computing. I vaguely knew the rules of the game, so I was able to set up a Go board on the pavement with two kinds of bullets. She played incredibly fast, but her head was definitely in the clouds.

Al was right, though. Meg's presence invigorated the male computers. All of them wanted to impress her, so they redoubled their various computational efforts.

At least three of the other computers approached her at various times but couldn't find the courage to spark up a conversation. It would only be a matter of time until they started interacting.

Whenever the weapons truck came through, I got plenty of supplies for the different computers and myself. The bed of shotgun shells was somewhat comfortable, but I couldn't get the chair completely constructed. I spent a lot of time writing about my experiences in the notebook, since I no longer needed it for Al's notes.

As another side project, I started transplanting some skullflowers into the yards in my cul-de-sac. They were kind of fun to have around and seemed to like living together. I had always been a terrible gardener on Earth, but skullflowers didn't need any supervision. They were already dead.

Between the computers and the skullflowers, my cul-de-sac started to draw attention from the other Suburbians. Some of them finally came of their houses to look around. I met a few people, but they rarely said much. A woman named Freda moved into the house across from mine, but she never talked to me, either.

On the negative side, my gunshot wounds still wouldn't heal. I was very aware of the holes and bullet fragments in my chest, especially when I forgot that I didn't need to breathe. I wore my spare shirt to cover things up, so at least I didn't look too gross on the outside.

Everything hurt more on days when I thought about Mallory. I could have used her help with some things.

One day, Satan came by one day to gloat about my situation. He laughed at my injuries, then called all the computers and flowers pathetic. I think he was actually a little mad, because he kicked over everyone's games and stormed off in a huff.

He must have really wanted my help on Earth, but wasn't much more he could do to me in Hell.

There was still a chance I might come back to life, but I wasn't counting on it. There was also the possibility Al would visit me, but I hoped he'd focus more on helping people who were still alive. I thought about sending him a postcard or letter, but he had never explained how it was done.

News from Earth was difficult to come by. New souls didn't head out to Suburbia for quite a while, and none of them were sociable, anyway. At some point I'd have to travel to The Big City to find out what was going on. Hopefully I'd get some good news.

When I'd been living in Suburbia for almost two months, Mallory showed up in my cul-de-sac, looking terrible. She had her arms folded, so I couldn't tell if her hand had grown back.

I was watching Meg play Go. I had learned a lot more about the game, but not enough to compete, especially at Meg's speed.

Mallory walked over, but I didn't acknowledge her.

"So these are your computers," she said. "What's this one doing?"

"Go," I said.

"I'm not going anywhere. I need to talk to you."

"No, she's playing Go. It's an ancient Chinese board game."

"Oh, I see." She watched for a few seconds. "It looks complicated."

"It is. Combinatorially speaking, she's got a long road ahead of her."

"Yeah, I bet."

I stood up to talk to Mallory. If she was tired before, now she was beyond exhausted. It looked like she hadn't slept since the last time I'd seen her.

I could see all the bones in her face under the huge black circles beneath her eyes. Her hair was falling out in several places. She still kept her arms crossed.

"So, um, what happened to you?" I asked.

"Well, your nemesis shot my hand off and broke my ankle. I sort of scraped around for a couple of days until my ankle healed up enough for me to walk.

"I was going to come find you, but then the dreams started, and they never let up. The more I thought about you, the worse they got. Eventually, I tried to get as far away from you as possible, so I headed for the boundary."

She shook her head. "It didn't help. I'm dreaming all the time now. It doesn't matter what I'm doing; I just fall asleep where I'm standing. I had to do something.

"Then I remembered that the dreams weren't as bad when I was helping you. I actually got to rest a little. I started thinking about helping you again, and I relaxed, just a bit.

"So I started walking back from the outskirts. It was a lot harder in than leaving. Time sort of stretched out. Between the walk and the dreams, I feel like it's been years since the last time I was here. How long has it been for you?"

"Maybe eight or nine weeks."

Mallory sighed. "Well, you seem to be in good spirits."

I shrugged. "I'm doing okay, I guess. My gunshot wounds are really acting up today."

She held up her right arm. It ended at the wrist, where several bone fragments were sticking out.

"Mine hasn't healed either."

I frowned. "Well, I held onto your old hand for you, but it started decomposing. I had to put it in the compost heap because of the odor." The compost heap consisted mostly of extra ammunition and Mallory's hand.

"I don't need it. This wound should heal eventually. It's just ... deep."

"I know."

Mallory took a deep breath. "I have to ask you something. After Al shot me, he took the bracelet back to you. Why?"

"Because he's my best friend."

"Then why did you let him have it?"

"The same reason."

She shook her head. "I could never do that." I saw a tear forming in her eye. "If I had gone back, I would just have killed Cody and ended up here again. Nothing would have changed, except the millions of people he helped would suffer. In spite of everything, he helped people and I didn't. That's why I'm here."

She blinked back her tears. "But I can still help you. If nothing else, I can stop these dreams." Mallory held out her remaining hand, which held two quarters. "I don't shoot as well with my left hand, but I was still able to threaten two people into giving me quarters. Along with your two, we have enough to make a phone call."

I took the quarters and pocketed them.

"Thanks, but now that Al's gone, I don't have anyone to call." I paused. "Actually, there's one person who might be willing to help."

"Another damned soul?"

"No, she's a succubus I met in the office. Her name is Bordella."

Mallory laughed. "You think a succubus is going to help you?"

"She said she would."

"Fine. It's your money."

Mallory led me to the nearest pay phone, a few blocks away. Just like before, I went inside and she squeezed in next to me.

"Any idea what her number is?" she said. "We don't have enough money to use the directory."

"Well, I had her number on my cell phone, but the battery died."

"Naturally."

"That's okay, it was easy to remember. It's all fives."

Mallory stared at me. "You're telling me this demoness gave you the number (555) 555-5555?" She closed her eyes and shook her head. "How can you be that gullible?"

"I don't think she was lying. She seemed pretty nice."

"Whatever you say. Like I told you, it's your dollar. I'm not going to find you any more quarters, though."

I inserted my quarters and picked up the handset. When I heard the dial tone, I pressed the "5" button ten times. It started ringing.

"At least it's a real number," I said.

Mallory still looked skeptical. After five rings, someone picked up and a woman's voice said, "Hello?"

"Hello. Is this Bordella?"

"Speaking. Who is this?" I smiled triumphantly. Mallory frowned and got out of the phone booth, leaving the door open.

"This is Doug DeWitt. I wanted to take you up on your offer to help."

"I see. I'll be right there." She hung up without saying anything else.

I put the handset back and turned to leave the booth.

To my surprise, Bordella was right there, pointing a large, violent-looking shotgun directly at my chest. She was clearly agitated. Her tiny bat wings were flapping uselessly.

"Damn it, Didi, do you have any idea what you've done?"

Before I could respond, she shot me point-blank with both barrels. As I slumped to the floor, I groaned.

"Why does this keep happening to me?"

Chapter Thirty-Eight

As soon as I got home from visiting Tina, I went online and downloaded the application to visit Hell. There wasn't any additional information on the site, just forms with the typical blanks like Name, Address, Phone Number, Age, Gender, Household Income, and Religious Affiliation.

Of course, I had to write down who I was visiting and why. The form also included a few open-ended questions like "Why do bad things happen to good people?"

When I finished, I was supposed to mail the paperwork to a P.O. Box in Oregon. The whole process was a little dubious, but Tina had seemed to know what she was talking about.

As I waited for a response, I started work on the environmental initiative for my company and continued raising money for the Pollinator Project. Once I got the necessary information from Al, I could begin the project for real.

I was starting to think the whole thing was a hoax when I finally got a letter in the mail. The envelope had no return address or stamp, but somehow it had made it to my mailbox anyway.

Inside the envelope was a single piece of letter paper. It had one line of type, printed at the very top of the page: "Your application to visit Hell has been accepted. Please arrive at our Des Moines office on June 1st, 2012 at 9:00 a.m. sharp. — Mgmt."

The appointment was still a few weeks away, but I started preparing well immediately. I bought a brand-new backpack and loaded it with food, water, and clothes, as well as a few other things that might come in handy. For entertainment, I packed some books.

Most importantly, I took a large, blank notebook so I could get as much information from Al as possible.

A few days before my appointment, I had to set up some long-term arrangements. Because I didn't know how long my visit trip would take, I told my boss I'd be taking an indefinite hiatus.

"In other words, you quit," he said. "That's fine. This environmental crap's just going to blow over anyway. Once that happens, we won't need you sticking your nose into everyone else's business."

Instead of responding, I just walked out. There was no reason to argue.

My rent and utilities were paid through the end of June and I didn't have any other obligations. I made sure to turn off all my electronics and locked the door when I left.

My final destination was a large office building in downtown Des Moines. All I knew was the office number and the building's address, so I drove down the day before my appointment to check it out.

Once I had a vague idea where I was supposed to go, I found a nearby hotel and stayed there overnight.

The next morning, I parked my station wagon in a long-term parking garage at and walked to the office building, showing up around 8:45.

Hell's central office was on the first floor of the building, hidden in a maze of featureless hallways. I finally found it after a good ten minutes of searching.

Besides the sign reading "Office No. 1119," there was no other identifying information. The truth was, I had no idea what to expect. The door was unlocked, so I went inside.

The office was brightly lit and completely empty. I conceded to myself that I had expected a bit more than an empty office.

A million doubts started running through my head as I realized just how gullible I had been. It wasn't even a very elaborate prank. After all, any website could pretend to represent Hell and anyone could rent a P.O. Box.

I had no job and no hope. If nothing else, I could abandon my stupid endeavor without losing anything more.

Right before I turned to leave, I noticed a tiny silver plaque on the opposite wall. I walked over to check it out, just in case.

It read, "To enter Hell, touch this panel."

I took a deep breath and touched the metal with my index finger. Everything went black. I felt a rush of hot wind all around me. A second later, my vision returned.

I was in exactly the same place, but now the plaque said, "Have a seat and wait to be called in."

I turned around and saw a much larger room full of uncomfortable chairs and depressed souls. I sat down in the nearest chair and started waiting.

I didn't like how the day was going so far, but I still held out some hope.

Chapter Thirty-Nine

After I collapsed, Bordella dragged me out of the phone booth and sat me up against it. Mallory watched, wide-eyed. She ran over to help, but Bordella just pointed in her direction and said, "Sleep." Mallory dropped to the ground and started snoring. Bordella sat down across from me, cross-legged.

"I've been waiting to shoot you for quite a while," she said. "It felt good."

I was having a hard time ignoring the pain or thinking, but I asked, "Why?"

She avoided the question. "You still don't know who I am, do you? That's probably why you got a 'D' in my class." She took a deep breath. "On Earth, you knew me as Dr. Celestina Cherry, Ph.D."

"That doesn't make any sense." I leaned forward and squinted at her face. On closer inspection, she bore more than a passing resemblance to Tina. "You're serious, aren't you?"

I leaned back. "I can't believe I didn't recognize you. Then again, you weren't as, um, zaftig back then. Or purple."

"It comes with the office."

"Did you become a demoness after Al died?"

"No, I was always a demoness. The management sent me to Earth to make sure Alphonse Bloom never did anything important. I followed him around through the years, making sure his career was mediocre. Every time he got close to doing something that benefitted mankind, I had to stop him. Not to brag, but I did pretty good job."

"I'd say so."

"He was supposed to start doing evil, though. Just a little here and there, but it would eventually make a big difference. I had a lot of potential plans, from computer viruses to biological weapons to killer robots."

She smiled for a split second. "That one was a little farfetched. Anyway, I was well on the way to fulfilling my mission when Al proposed to me. I knew it might happen, but I still wasn't ready, so I made some excuses and ran away.

"I thought I could take some time to think it over. After all, how could he have fallen in love with me after everything I did to him? It didn't make sense.

"Then something funny happened. As soon as I left, Al went to his best friend for help. Instead of being a pliable dumbass, you took charge and told him off. Unfortunately, you also told him the truth. He didn't respond very well to that. I should have gone back to check on him, but I was afraid."

I coughed. "Afraid of what?"

"I was afraid that I loved him. If I did, my job would be impossible. I couldn't force myself to go back, and that one moment of weakness gave him enough time to kill himself. Then it was all over. My assignment was terminated; I had to come back here to do clerical work.

"Imagine my surprise when you came through my office. I'll be honest, I never thought you had the guts to get this far. Then, a few weeks ago, I was even more surprised when Al came through. He didn't recognize me, either."

She shook her head. "I warned you not to lose your visitor's pass, Didi." She laughed. "Of course, he claimed you gave it to him."

"Actually, I did."

"Bullshit." She stared at me. "Seriously? There's no reason to do that. I just can't believe ..." She trailed off.

"Anyway, the management is still sorting things out, but we're almost ready to send him back to Earth now. It isn't easy to undo history, even after eight months. The whole thing is a bureaucratic nightmare."

"When he gets back, will he be able to prevent me from going to Hell?"

"No. Nothing's going to change down here. You're still going to die at 9 a.m. on June 1st, no matter what. You'll just drop dead wherever you are. At least you've got your hobbies, right?"

"Right." I hadn't been too hopeful, but now I knew I was here for good. Unless, of course, someone visited me.

"As for me, whenever the management sends Al back, I'm going back, too. He's not going to shoot himself this time. I'm going to marry him, and then I'll have to corrupt him all over again. It's going to be much harder this time."

"Why?"

"Because he's been to Hell, of course. He knows what's in store for him, so he's going to try much harder to avoid it. I'll have to be a lot more subtle." She gazed off for a second. "Maybe I can convince him it was all just a dream."

"I meant, why do you have to corrupt him?"

"It's my job. If I don't do it, I'll get punished."

"How?"

She shrugged. "I'd have to do clerical work."

"What happens when you finish the assignment?"

"I'll probably get to enjoy myself on Earth for a while, then I'll come back here and do clerical work."

"If the end result's the same, then why bother? When you go back, can't you just love him instead of corrupting him?"

Bordella got flustered again. "Love? I don't know how to do that.

201

I'm a succubus."

"It sounds like you've already started. Besides, what makes you think humans know what they're doing? Al never did. I certainly don't."

"Obviously."

"My point is, you can do more with your life. If you help Al instead of corrupting him, who knows what might happen?"

"You could be right." She stood back up.

"Anyway, I wanted to thank you in addition to shooting you. It'll be nice to go back to Earth. Honestly, the nicest part is being with Al." She reached into her cleavage and pulled out another visitor's pass.

"I stole this pass for you. There was no reason not to, since I'm already fired." She knelt down and snapped the bracelet on my wrist, a little more delicately this time. "I have no idea what comes next, but I'll see you on the other side."

In a puff of black smoke, she was gone.

I suddenly felt a lot better. I looked at my torso and saw a reassuring lack of bullet holes. I walked over to Mallory and shook her. Instead of jerking awake, she just opened her eyes and sighed.

"I didn't have any dreams," she said. "It was wonderful." She sat up and steadied herself with her right hand, then stared at it. "Wait. When did my hand grow back?"

"I'm not sure. My gunshot wounds are gone, too. It's kind of nice."

"No shit." She looked at my wrist and noticed my visitor's pass. "You got another pass?" Her eyes flashed for a second, then she relaxed. "I think you should get out of here as soon as you can. That thing is dangerous."

"I know. I just wanted to tell you that I really appreciated your help."

"You're welcome."

She got up, and we walked back to my cul-de-sac together.

I said goodbye to everyone. Most of the computers pretended to ignore me, but I could tell they heard.

The skullflowers were equally nonchalant. Most of them had considered becoming humans again, so I'd played the name-guessing game with about half of them. Maybe they'd try to do more eventually.

Mallory looked at everything and actually smiled. "This isn't so bad," she said. "I can keep an eye on it for you. I'll still have to travel around, but at least I can always come back here."

"I know the computers will appreciate it. Maybe you can help the skullflowers, too."

"I'll do what I can." She looked me in the eyes. "By the way, I read that book you gave me. I'd never even heard of Emily Dickinson. It turns out she hardly did anything during her life, but after she died, her writing helped people.

"I was thinking, maybe my life doesn't have to end with death. Maybe I can still help people now that I'm dead."

I smiled. "You should try it. I think you can make good use of this time. If nothing else, you'll be able to sleep."

"True." She thought for a second. "Does it count as doing good when you do it for selfish reasons?"

"I think it counts as doing good when you do good."

Mallory nodded. "Makes sense to me. Anyway, I'm going to sleep." She went into Al's former house and slammed the door.

I waved after her, then headed out. I walked out of Suburbia toward the gray horizon. I wasn't sure where which direction led to the exact center of Hell, but I tried to approximate.

In the end, it didn't matter, because I found myself at the central office after about ten minutes. It looked exactly like the office building in Des Moines.

The front door led into the large waiting room where I arrived. Except for the new batch of freshly damned souls, everything was the

203

same, including the receptionist. She waved me up to the desk.

"Are you all done with your visit, Mr. DeWitt?" she said.

"I think I am."

"Then you're free to go."

"Excellent." I looked around. "How do I leave?"

"The same way you came in: just touch the metal plate on the wall. It won't work without a visitor's pass, though."

"I see." I walked over to the plate and pressed my right index finger against it. This time, there was a white flash and a cool breeze.

When my vision returned, I was standing in the empty office in Des Moines. My bracelet was gone; so was the metal plaque.

I still had my backpack, but the only thing left inside was the notebook full of stories about Hell. Everything else had just vanished.

I started to feel lightheaded. I couldn't figure out why, until I realized that I hadn't breathed yet. I gasped for air and tried to get back in the habit of inhaling and exhaling.

I left the office and made my way back to the front of the building. As I walked, I thought about all the things I needed to do. I got a little overwhelmed, but after a second or two, I was able to suppress it.

I wouldn't be alone. My best friend would be there to help, and maybe we could even convince a certain succubus to assist us.

If nothing else, I had friends in Hell, so there really was nothing to worry about. When I reached the front door, I was truly hopeful.

I took a deep breath, went outside, and faced the day.

Epilogue

Dr. Alphonse Bloom, Nobel Lecture 2018

I'd like to start by saying that being awarded the Nobel Peace Prize is the strangest thing that has ever happened to me. Only those who know me personally can truly appreciate that statement. Don't get me wrong, I'm thrilled to be recognized for a Nobel Prize. The strange part is how I got here.

First of all, I should point out that computer scientists are rarely acknowledged for our contributions, even though at this point, every science is computer science.

Current advances in physics, chemistry, and medicine would be impossible without computers. Considering how much computers can do, it's sometimes easy to forget that those discoveries are made by people.

Those who suggest that scientists and doctors can be replaced with computers are extremely misguided. Computers are not people, and no matter how advanced technology may become, human beings will always be better at certain things, especially creative endeavors.

Some would say that makes artificial intelligence a futile effort. I take the opposite view.

Our goal as computer scientists is not to make miniature humans. After all, making miniature humans isn't very difficult. Just ask my lovely wife, Dr. Celestina Cherry-Bloom, and our two kids, Michael and Gabriel.

Without Tina's tireless support, I would never have come this far. Seriously, folks, she's an angel.

In reality, computer scientists work to understand the world by making our own. We call it "artificial" intelligence because we started from scratch. Naturally, that's why computers are so different from us. It's also why they can do so many things we can't.

Once we determined their true potential, the existence of computers changed every aspect of human life. The world would be a better place if humans could realize their true potential so well.

As scientists, we all have to ask ourselves some difficult questions. Here's one of mine: "Has the existence of computers made the world a better place?" The answer is a resounding "Maybe."

Computers have the remarkable ability to do two contradictory things at the same time. They bring people together and isolate them. They educate people but do all the thinking for them. They help people work yet prevent them from working.

Like so many other things, computers are a part of the modern world, for better or worse. Because of that, I used to think that my contributions were arbitrary. No matter what I did, the world would stay roughly the same.

In other words, I was asking myself the wrong question. When I finally realized that, I found a new one: "How can I use computers to make the world a better place?"

Once I decided that it was my responsibility to improve the world, I had to go out and do it. The trouble was, I had no idea how. There are so many problems in the world, how could I possibly fix them all?

When I contemplated the enormity of the world's problems, I felt completely powerless. Instead of thinking about the entire world, I started paying attention to the effect I had on the people around me, and I never felt more powerful.

I discovered that my actions have the power to make people happy or sad. When I say something polite, I make people feel good. If I'm rude or indifferent, I might ruin someone's entire day. Of course, I can also turn someone's day around with a smile. Even my smallest actions have a profound effect.

It's easy to complain about the evils of the world, but evil's most common form is inaction. The truth is, not doing evil isn't enough. You also have to do good.

Of course, doing good is difficult sometimes. You might have to honestly ask yourself, "What's in it for me?" and honestly answer, "Nothing."

You'll never be able to combat all the evil in the entire world, but if you fight it a little every day, you'll be amazed how much the world changes, all thanks to your tremendous power.

That revelation is what ultimately brought me here today, even though I started small.

From its humble beginnings in 2011, the Pollinator Project has become a true force for good. When it began, we had an attainable goal and a clear means of achieving it. The hardest part was taking action, and believe me, it was hard.

None of this would have been possible without my colleague and best friend, Doug DeWitt. No one has worked harder than he has.

Doug spent the last six years managing the Pollinator Project, turning it from a single office in Akron to more than 60 across the world. He also spent three years developing the polymers necessary to create our nanomachines. I honestly don't know how he does it.

Our project brought together hundreds of scientists from a wide variety of disciplines, from entomology to materials science to economics. The process became so complicated even I couldn't keep track of it all. For the uninitiated, I'll try to explain it anyway.

We started by managing the bees we already had by studying and combating colony collapse disorder. We also began experimenting with materials and software to manufacture nanomachines that could find and transport pollen. Once manufacturing began, we were able to distribute our bees and bots to troubled locations almost immediately.

Over the past three years, we've found a way to pollinate more than 90% of the world's crops, including some whose natural pollinators are nearly extinct. Between pollinator management and nanomachines, we revolutionized agriculture.

There are now 7.5 billion people on this planet, and thanks to the Pollinator Project, they all have access to food. I'm confident when I say that the world is a better place today than it was when we started, but we aren't done yet.

This year, we began some revolutionary new research on water purification. With any luck, my sons will grow up in a world where fresh water will be available on every part of the globe.

Of course, I was never alone. If I could share my medal equally among everyone involved, the pieces would be even smaller than my pollinators.

In addition to Doug, Tina, and my sons, I have to thank my parents, whose investment advice helped us increase our funds tenfold the first year.

I also want to thank the Pollinator Project's hundreds of employees, particularly Jeff Silvey, Karen Hartke, and Kathy Rebarber, who have been with us since the very beginning.

I owe a special thanks to Cody Costello, who used his international influence to bring attention to this problem. Without his help, we would never have been able to earn the love and support of so many volunteers worldwide. Unfortunately, he went missing in Iowa earlier this year. Today, I'm wearing a Cody Pendant in his honor.

My wife, truly a lady and scholar, once told me that morality is what we choose to do; it's never automatic. It held a special meaning for me because computers don't make choices. They aren't good or evil at all, and without our direction, computers are completely lost.

That's why it's our responsibility to make them a force for good in the world. I've done that.

On the other hand, I've been lost myself a few times. Without the help of my friends and family, my life would be meaningless. I could never be more grateful for that. I want to take this opportunity to thank them and everyone else in my life.

Thank you very, very much.